Christmas Custard Conspiracy

The Drunken Pie Café Cozy Mysteries, Book Six

Diana DuMont

CHAPTER ONE

"You need to move it a little to the left," I said as I squinted up at the bright red bow that was outlined in glittery golden trim. The streetlights on Main Street caught the bow's glittery edges and sent patterns of iridescent shimmers dancing across the sidewalk in front of the First Bank of Sunshine Springs. I sighed happily as I thought about how festive everything looked. Today was only the first day of December, but my first Christmas in Sunshine Springs was already shaping up to be a truly joyful experience.

High above me, Theo Russo sighed as well—but his sigh was not a happy one. He glared down at me from his perch on the top rung of a fifteen foot ladder. "Izzy, you told me I needed to move it a little to the right. I did, and now you're telling me to move it to the left. Which is it? Make up your mind."

I smiled up at him, unbothered by his grumpiness. "You moved it too far to the right. So now you need to move it a little back. Just a bit. Yes, just like that! Right there! Stop! Perfect!"

Beside me, my Dalmatian, Sprinkles, barked in agreement. The bow was finally positioned perfectly in the center of the First Bank sign. Theo grumbled as he secured the bow in place, but when he finally climbed down the ladder and looked up at the bow, he cracked a smile.

"I've got to hand it to you, Izzy. You're really good at this. I bet I couldn't have gotten that bow centered more perfectly if I'd measured it down to the centimeter."

I grinned as I reached down to give Sprinkles a good rub behind the ears. "I had lots of practice when I was putting up decorations inside the café. And speaking of the café, let's hurry and finish hanging the rest of these decorations so we can go back there and have some pie. I've got a freshly baked cranberry vodka crumble with our name on it.

Theo's smile widened. "I knew there was a reason I volunteered to join you on the decorating committee."

He winked at me, then hoisted the ladder up on his shoulder and headed down to the next sign that we had been assigned to decorate. My face heated slightly as I scurried after him, and I knew I was blushing. Theo was always winking at me in that flirtatious way, and I'd learned to ignore it for the most part. But something about the festive atmosphere and twinkling lights made his winks seem even more romantic than usual, and I was having a hard time ignoring them as resolutely as I normally did.

I should have known that volunteering to put up Main Street Christmas decorations with Theo would lead to moments like this. In the short time that I'd been living in Sunshine Springs, he'd made countless attempts to convince me to date him. I'd always pushed him away, and I had no intentions of changing my mind about that anytime soon.

But the twinkling lights could really get to a girl.

I sighed again as Theo, mercifully oblivious to the thoughts swirling around in my head, shouted at me to dig another bow out of the giant black trash bag of bows I was carrying. I did as I was told, and handed it to him as he once again started climbing his ladder, this time to put a bow atop the sign outside of the law offices of J.J. Dunham and Associates.

I couldn't help but smile as I peered into the window of the dark offices. I had been a lawyer once, but that felt like a lifetime ago. After a nasty divorce, I'd given up my law practice in San Francisco for the chance to start over and follow my dreams of opening a café. I now ran the Drunken Pie Café, where locals and wine country tourists alike could stop by for espresso drinks, glasses of wine, and freshly baked pies—many of which were boozy pies, infused with various types of wine, beer, or liquor.

My café was keeping me crazily busy during the holiday season, when many tourists were making their way through wine country, doing wine tastings and stocking up on bottles of wine to give as gifts or to serve during their upcoming holiday dinners. Yet in the midst of all the business, I'd still been determined to help decorate Sunshine Springs. This was my new hometown now, and I was determined to be an involved citizen.

"How's this?" Theo called down, breaking into my thoughts once again. I peered up at the bow, squinting as I carefully assessed its positioning.

"A little to the left. Just a *little*. Don't go moving it half a foot and then yelling at me because I tell you to move it back to the right. A little means a little."

Theo rolled his eyes at me, but he was much more careful about how far he moved the bow this time. After a few more slight adjustments, he managed to get the bow in what I thought was the perfect position. As he secured it, I reached down to rub Sprinkles' ears again. My Dalmatian whined quietly, and I knew he was getting impatient with this whole decorating process. He wanted to head back to the café, where he could give me sweet puppy eyes and convince me to spare a slice of pie for him.

"Only a few more signs," I promised.

And it was true. The bag of bows I was holding was nearly empty, and Main Street was starting to look like a true Christmas wonderland. Theo and I had already hung lighted garlands all up and down the street. Ornaments in jewel-tones adorned those garlands, and here and there a poinsettia plant or a wooden reindeer had been strategically placed. The bows were the finishing touch, and we'd almost hung all of them. I felt a puff of pride when I thought about how I had helped transform our town's little city center. It might not be as fancy as some of the Christmas displays back in San Francisco, but it was home.

Theo must have thought the same thing. I watched as he also looked up and down the street from his vantage point on the ladder. "It looks amazing, if I do say so myself."

I grinned at him, and couldn't help but notice how handsome he looked in the soft glow of the lighted garlands. Too bad I wasn't looking for a man right now, because he was a catch. He was the handsomest man in Sunshine Springs, and the wealthiest. He owned the Sunshine Springs Winery, which was what had put this little Northern California town on the map, and pretty much every single woman in town would have married him in a heartbeat.

Naturally, he chose to fall for me, the one girl who was determined *not* to date him. That was small town life, though, wasn't it? What would Sunshine Springs be without a couple of complicated love stories?

"You're despicable! A true disgrace to humanity!"

I jumped, startled as an angry voice cut through the peaceful quiet. Sprinkles let out a low growl, and we both whipped around to look in the direction the voice had come from. When I saw who was yelling, I groaned.

"What is Vinny doing out here?" I asked.

"Causing trouble, no doubt," Theo said as he climbed down from the ladder. "Who is he yelling at?"

I squinted in Vinny's direction, trying to see if I could make out the unlucky recipient of the tirade. Whomever Vinny was yelling at, however, was facing away from me. All I could tell was that the person was tall, appeared to be male, and was wearing a long-sleeved plaid shirt.

Vinny Herron, on the other hand, I could see clearly. He was facing my direction and stood directly under a streetlamp, which illuminated his shaggy brown hair, tanned leathery skin, and dark brown eyes. He wasn't that tall—in fact, he stood a good foot lower than the person he was yelling at. But what Vinny lacked in height he made up for in pluck. He was holding a large wooden picket sign that proclaimed "Christmas kills trees!" in bright red letters. I watched as he shoved the sign into the other man's face and resumed yelling.

"You're ruining the environment, you know that? You're not spreading joy. You're spreading destruction!"

Theo had climbed all the way down the ladder now, and I heard him exhale in frustration beside me. "That fool is always causing a scene."

I grunted my agreement. Vinny Herron was a longtime resident of Sunshine Springs, but it was only recently that he'd decided to become a champion of environmental issues. I had done quite a bit of conservation work myself when I lived in San Francisco, and I agreed with Vinny that we should protect our natural resources as much as possible.

What I didn't agree with were his methods, which usually involved a lot of yelling, much of it nonsensical. Often, as was now the case, he also carried around a big sign to shove in people's faces, just in case his yelling didn't get the point across. At that moment, I watched in horror as he literally whacked the other man over the head with the sign.

"He's out of his mind!" I gasped. Sprinkles started barking, then followed Theo as he started running down the street toward the two men.

"You're killing the earth with your stupid Christmas decorations!" Vinny yelled as he hit the man with the sign again. "You're not spreading cheer, you're spreading death!"

The other man fell to the ground, shielding his head with his hands. "You're out of your mind, Vinny! I'm going to sue you for assault! Why don't you go plant a tree instead of running around yelling at people?"

I saw then that the man Vinny was beating was none other than Simon Farrington. Simon's claim to fame in Sunshine Springs was that he had won the city's decorating contest for as many years as people could remember. Every year, in an effort to build community pride and foster holiday spirit, the city council offered a generous five thousand dollar prize to the contest winner. The prize was worth it to the city because the elaborate Christmas decorations on many Sunshine Springs homes drew in plenty of tourists, who would ooh and ahh at the displays and then would open their wallets to buy food, wine, and souvenirs. For Sunshine Springs, a town that depended on tourist dollars to survive, the contest was serious business.

And for Simon Farrington, the defending champion of the contest, there was no way that a crazy man with a sign was going to hold him back from decorating and winning his prize money.

"Leave me alone, you fool!" Simon yelled, pushing up from where he had fallen and pushing back against Vinny and his sign.

Vinny raised the sign again, ready to make another attempt at smashing Simon's face in with it. I winced as I watched the scene unfolding in front of me. The festive ambience was completely ruined, and, worse, tourists were starting to creep out of the nearby restaurants, curious to see what all of the commotion was about. This was not the sort of publicity that we needed for our town.

Before Vinny could manage to get another hit in on Simon, though, Theo reached the two of them and pulled Vinny back. Sprinkles rushed around the three men, barking excitedly as Simon slowly stood and Vinny tried unsuccessfully to break free of Theo's iron grip.

"Calm down, Vinny," Theo urged. "You're just making a fool of yourself."

"I will not calm down!" Vinny shrieked out. "Not while everyone in this town insists on cutting down trees to decorate! Why must we kill trees to celebrate?"

"Actually, the local tree farms are all committed to replanting trees to replace the ones they sell," one of the nearby tourists spoke up in a chipper voice.

Vinny was not impressed by this fun fact, and turned to scream at the tourist. The tourist, looking like he feared for his life, rushed back inside one of the restaurants. Simon started to yell something else, but Theo shook his head at him, still holding Vinny back.

"Simon, just get out of here," Theo said in that commanding voice of his. I'd seen him take control of several situations in the time I'd been here in Sunshine Springs, and still it amazed me how everyone stopped and listened when he spoke in that tone. Tonight was no different. Simon looked for one moment like he might protest, but then thought better of it and clamped his mouth shut. With an airy toss of his head, Simon sauntered away, mumbling something about crazy tree huggers.

"I'm not crazy! You're crazy, if you think we can all keep wasting earth's resources like this."

"That's enough," Theo bellowed to Vinny. In response, Vinny did stop yelling at Simon, and instead turned angry eyes on Theo.

"Hey, aren't you the one decorating Main Street? You should be ashamed of yourself as well. Those decorations are all unnecessary. You're killing the earth, too."

Vinny reached to try to raise his sign again, presumably to hit Theo over the head. But Vinny never stood a chance. Theo was twice as strong as him, and was starting to resemble an angry bear.

"I'm not killing anything," Theo roared. "For one thing, these decorations are things the city already owns and has owned for years. They are reusable and aren't causing any damage to the environment. For another thing, I am not in the mood to be hit over the head by the likes of you. I'm giving you about five seconds to get out of here before I hit you back, and trust me, you are not going to like it if I hit back."

I watched in fascination as Vinny considered Theo's words for a split-second, then dropped his sign and ran off into the darkness. Theo kicked the sign angrily and cursed, then seemed to notice that many of the tourists were still watching him.

"My apologies," he said to them stiffly. "That man is a bit overzealous and misguided, but he's gone now. Please, go back to enjoying your dinners."

The tourists continued to gawk at Theo for a few more moments, but then they all turned to head back into the restaurants from which they'd come. Sprinkles settled down and stopped barking, and I walked over to where Theo was standing, looking quite flustered. I reached out a tentative hand and put it on his forearm.

"Hey, you look stressed. Maybe we should save the last couple bows for later and go ahead to the café to have some pie. A break might do us both good."

Theo's face was nearly purple with rage, and I could tell he was taking deep breaths to try to calm down. For a moment, I thought he wasn't going to agree, but then he nodded.

"That's a good idea. I shouldn't lose my temper like that, but I'm worried that Vinny is too far out of control. He's going to ruin Christmas in Sunshine Springs if he keeps causing scenes."

"Nonsense," I chided as I pulled Theo toward my café. "He's just one person. He's not going to ruin Christmas." I gestured toward the beautiful decorations on Main Street. "What could possibly ruin Christmas in a place as beautiful as this?"

Theo only grunted in response, and I couldn't ignore the shiver that ran through my body. I wanted to believe that this was going to be the most magical Christmas I'd ever had, but was I being naïve? Was it going to take more than tinsel and lights to hold back the trouble brewing beneath the surface in Sunshine Springs?

CHAPTER TWO

Once inside the Drunken Pie Café, the stress of watching the fight between Simon and Vinny melted away. How could anyone be stressed when assailed with the delicious aromas of freshly baked pie, buttery lattes, and spicy wine? Not to mention, the inside of the café looked like a winter wonderland. With twinkling lights, glittery snowflake decorations, and plenty of deep green pine garlands, my café had never looked quite so joyful. Through the window, one could even see that the giant wooden "Drunken Pie Café" sign outside my front door was covered in snow. The snow wasn't real, of course. Northern California wine country wasn't exactly known for white Christmases, with its mild winter weather. But I'd found faux snow that looked startlingly realistic, and I was pleased with the wintry effect it gave my pie shop.

Theo visibly relaxed as he entered the café, and I let out a small sigh of relief. Theo was usually so easygoing that seeing him all riled up always felt disconcerting. I'd been worried that the encounter with the two men fighting in the street would leave him riled up all night, but the smell of pie and the twinkle of the café lights seemed to put him at ease.

"Eggnog bourbon pie? Or cranberry vodka crumble? I've got both freshly baked."

Theo scrunched his face up in thought, as though choosing which pie to eat was the most important decision he'd made all day. Unlikely, since he ran a huge winery and was surely making important decisions constantly. But he did look adorable as he seriously considered which of my pies to eat.

"Eggnog bourbon, I think."

"Good choice." I nodded in approval. "It's been selling quite well, and it might end up being the most popular of my special holiday flavors. Want some wine with it?"

I held up a bottle of Theo's 2016 Pinot, which was one of the most popular wines I served in my café. It paired well with numerous flavors of pie, and several customers had told me today that it was excellent with the eggnog bourbon pie. But Theo was shaking his head.

"I've had enough wine today. One of my employees called in sick so I helped man the tasting room for a while. I always help myself to plenty of wine when I'm working in the tasting room, but today I was especially generous with myself." Theo laughed and shook his head. "It was a good day at work, that's for sure. But I don't think I should drink anymore today. Got any decaf coffee?"

I grinned. "Oh, is the winery owner a lightweight?"

Theo rolled his eyes at me. "Not a lightweight. Just not an idiot. I'm not a fan of wine hangovers."

"Calm down," I tsked. "I'm just giving you a hard time. Of course I have decaf coffee. I also have hot chocolate, if you're interested in something a little sweeter."

Theo groaned and looked down at his stomach, grabbing at nonexistent love handles. "I shouldn't add hot chocolate on top of pie. I can already feel the holiday weight gain creeping up on me."

"But my hot chocolate is so good," I countered.

"Your hot chocolate is good," Theo agreed as he sank into one of the café chairs in defeat. "Alright. Hot chocolate and eggnog bourbon pie it is."

I laughed at his dramatics, then began preparing his treats. I refrained from telling him that he didn't need to worry about gaining weight. He was one of the fittest people in Sunshine Springs, and it would take more than one little slice of pie and mug of hot chocolate to make his clothes too small. But if I made comments like this, I knew he'd tease me about admiring him, and hint at the fact that I should date him.

I was *not* going to fall for him just because the Christmas season was so romantic.

The Christmas season was also busy, and I had a lot of pie to bake and sell. Not to mention I had parties to attend and gift exchanges to shop for. I was throwing myself fully into the holiday festivities in Sunshine Springs. This was my first small-town Christmas, and I was determined to make it count.

As for Sprinkles, he seemed determined to cause a ruckus. Unlike Theo and I, he had not relaxed the moment we walked into the café. Instead, he'd started pacing nervously back and forth. At first, I'd thought he was worried that I wasn't going to give him any pie. But even after I'd assured him that I'd find a slice of non-boozy pie for him, he'd continued to pace. Now, he stood at the glass front door of the café, pressing wet nose-prints into the door and barking.

"Sprinkles! You know better than that. I'm going to have to clean all your little nose-smears off that door before opening tomorrow! Get back over here or I'm not giving you any pie."

Sprinkles looked guiltily back at me, and for a moment I thought he was going to ignore me. He could be quite stubborn when he was in the mood to be, but he had a hard time resisting pie. With a frustrated sigh, he left the window and came to sit by Theo. Even barking at the tourists wasn't worth the risk of losing pie.

Theo absentmindedly rubbed Sprinkles' ears as I began steaming milk for the hot chocolate.

"These decorations are great, Izzy, but you are missing one thing."

I arched an eyebrow at him from behind the stainless steel pitcher of milk that was rapidly warming. "Oh? I didn't realize you were such an expert on holiday décor."

Theo ignored my sarcasm. "You need mistletoe."

I rolled my eyes. "I most certainly do not. Why would I want to encourage people to start kissing in my pie shop?"

Theo wiggled his eyebrows at me, and then, in an off-key voice he started singing, "Silent night, romantic nighhhhht!"

As he dragged out the last word of the song, I threw a dish towel across the room at him. "You definitely had too much wine today. What's gotten into you?"

Before he could answer, Sprinkles was at the window, barking again.

"Sprinkles!" I chided. "Get away from the window and be quiet. I swear, I should kick both of you boys out of my café and just enjoy a slice of pie in peace and quiet by myself."

Theo merely threw back his head and laughed. He always found it amusing when he managed to make me flustered, which only made me more flustered. I took a few deep breaths and told myself not to let him get to me. Perhaps part of the problem was that Christmas on my own did make me feel a bit lonely, and a small part of me wanted to put up a sprig of mistletoe to give Theo an excuse to kiss me.

But only a small part. A bigger part of me had too much pride for those sorts of games. Reminding myself that I was busy with the café and other Christmas activities. I started to stir fresh cocoa powder and sugar into the steaming milk. But before I could make much progress on the hot chocolate, Sprinkles was at the door again, barking even louder than before.

"Sprinkles!" I exclaimed. "This is your last warning. Get away from the door, or no pie!"

But whatever Sprinkles was barking at must have interested him even more than pie, which was quite a feat. He ignored me and continued to bark, louder and faster with every passing second. Theo glanced back at the dog with a slight frown on his face, and I felt a sudden rush of embarrassment. I must look like a completely irresponsible pet owner who had no idea how to train a dog. In exasperation, I threw down the whisk I'd been using to stir the hot chocolate, sending little splatters of chocolatey milk across the counter.

"Sprinkles! What has gotten into you?"

I marched around the counter and to the door, where I grabbed him by his sparkly neon-green collar. The collar had been a gift from my Grams, who was obsessed with bright, neon colors. I hadn't been a big fan of the color, but Grams loved Sprinkles so much and was so helpful with watching him when I was busy at the café. I'd figured if she wanted to choose a special collar for him, I should just let her.

Now, I was glad for that collar. It was made of strong, high-quality leather, and it was easy to grip as I held onto it and used it to pull Sprinkles away from the door.

"That's about enough of that!" I told him in a severe tone. To my surprise, he looked up at me with defiance, then bolted for the door again. I hadn't been expecting that, and had loosened my grip on his collar just enough that he was able to escape my grasp and head back to the window, barking like crazy once more. I looked back at Theo and shrugged sheepishly, but felt more embarrassed than ever.

"He's usually not this bad," I said. "I don't know what's gotten into him."

Theo's frown had deepened, and to my surprise he was nodding slowly. "You're right. He's not usually quite this bad. What is he barking at?"

I threw my hands above my head in exasperation. "I don't know. Probably some drunken tourists or something. He always finds it really entertaining when they stumble down Main Street."

"Have you looked?"

I gritted my teeth together. "No. I'm sure it's nothing exciting. I've seen it all before. It is wine country, after all. People sometimes get a bit too excited and drink a bit too much wine."

Theo didn't look amused. He was slowly standing from his seat. "I've never heard him bark quite like that. I think something's wrong."

I was about to make a smart-aleck comment about how I knew my dog well and I would know if he was using his "something's wrong" bark. But then, it hit me. Sprinkles *was* using that bark. I'd been so irritated with him for misbehaving in front of Theo that I hadn't been paying attention. Feeling a growing sense of trepidation, I turned to look out the front door to see what Sprinkles was barking at. When I saw it, I gasped and clasped my hand over my mouth.

"Izzy?" Theo asked, concern filling his voice. In my peripheral vision, I could see him moving toward me, but I couldn't tear my eyes away from the scene in front of me.

"You were right," I managed to say. "Something is definitely wrong."

CHAPTER THREE

When Theo joined me at the window, he also clasped his hands over his mouth in shock. "Is that…?"

"Yes," I answered, knowing what he was asking without needing him to finish his sentence. "That's Simon. And he's not looking so good."

A few yards down from the Drunken Pie Café, in front of another Main Street shop known as "Moe's Souvenirs," Simon Farrington had been securely strapped to a street lamp using quite a bit of pine garland. His head was slumped forward, but since I was viewing him from the side I could see that it was definitely him. He wasn't moving, and his eyes were open and staring straight down at the ground below him.

"Is he…?" I couldn't bring myself to say the word, but Theo understood.

"Is he dead?" Theo completed the question for me. "I can't be certain from this distance, but it certainly looks like that's a possibility. We'd better go check on him."

Theo pushed the door to the café open, and Sprinkles immediately bounded out into the night, barking up a storm as he raced toward Simon's slumped figure.

"Sprinkles! Don't touch him!" I pleaded as I followed him out with Theo right beside me. Thankfully, Sprinkles actually listened to me for once, and stopped a few feet away from the streetlamp. He alternated between barking and growling, but Simon paid him no mind. If the man wasn't dead, he was definitely unconscious.

When we got closer, I gasped again as I realized that there was a length of pine garland around Simon's neck. It was just loose enough for me to see the bright red marks it had left, and I felt my stomach turn. Had someone used this pine garland to strangle him?

Theo took a deep breath and stepped forward, placing two fingers against Simon's neck. I had never been so thankful to have Theo with me, and I breathed a silent prayer of thanks that I hadn't had to be the one to check for a pulse.

After a few moments, Theo looked over at me and shook his head sadly. "He's gone. We better call Mitch."

I stared in shock at Simon's limp form. His eyes were wide and his lips were slightly parted, giving his face an overall expression of surprise. It seemed impossible that he could be dead. Hadn't I just seen him here, alive and well, arguing with Vinny?

The thought gave me pause, and I looked up at Theo. "Do you think Vinny did this?" I asked, my voice barely more than a whisper.

Theo's eyes looked dark as he pulled his cell phone from his pocket. "I don't know. They did seem rather displeased with each other, but it seems like a big jump to go from arguing about the environmental impact of Christmas decorations to strangling someone."

I didn't disagree with Theo there, but if it hadn't been Vinny, then who? Who had hated Simon enough to do something like this? True, Simon could be obnoxious, especially around this time of year when he was competing for the top prize in the Sunshine Springs decorating contest. But surely he hadn't been obnoxious enough for someone to actually want to murder him!

I sighed. From the looks of the slumped, lifeless form in front of me, he had. Sprinkles whined, and I reached down to rub his ear as Theo dialed Mitch's number.

"Sorry I didn't believe you, boy," I murmured. Sprinkles looked up at me sorrowfully, his eyes wide and alert. I got the feeling that he was worried that whoever had committed this crime might still be nearby, and that he feared for my safety. He wasn't exactly what you'd call a guard dog, but he was fiercely loyal, and I knew he would put up a good fight against anyone who tried to harm me.

I realized with a start that Sprinkles might have actually seen the whole murder happening. He might know who the perpetrator was!

"If only you could talk," I said to him. He gave me a few slow thumps of his tail, as if to agree.

By then, Theo had reached Mitch, and was explaining the odd situation we found ourselves in. I winced when I thought of Sheriff Mitchell McCoy, better known to everyone in Sunshine Springs as simply "Mitch."

When I'd first met Mitch, our friendship had gotten off to a rocky start. I'd just moved to town, and had been accused of murdering someone who had dropped dead of poison in front of my café—not the best way to start things off in a new town. Luckily, I'd been acquitted of that murder, and Mitch and I had become pretty close friends. In fact, he'd wanted to date me for a while, although it seemed that lately he'd had his eye on another café owner in town: my friend Alice Warner. Fine by me. Like I'd already told myself a hundred times tonight, I wasn't interested in dating anyone right now. Alice could have Mitch.

But although I was spending a bit less time around Mitch these days, thanks to the fact that he was always hanging out with Alice, I still knew the man quite well. And I knew he would not be happy to find me at the scene of another murder. He did his best to keep me from playing detective, and I was pretty sure he thought I showed up at these crime scenes on purpose. But I had enough to do right now getting all my holiday pie orders completed. I didn't have time to go looking for trouble.

I couldn't help it if trouble somehow always seemed to find me.

"Mitch is on his way," Theo said as he ended the call on his cell phone. "He said he's right down the street, so it shouldn't be more than a minute or two before he gets here. He's also called for some of his officers to come help him, since this appears to be a serious crime."

I took one more quick glance at Simon's body, then shuddered and looked away. I still couldn't believe that this was happening.

A low growl from Sprinkles drew my attention, and I looked in the direction he was gazing to see several tipsy tourists making their way down the sidewalk in our direction.

"Uh-oh," Theo murmured. "Here comes trouble."

The tourists, a group of middle-aged women, giggled and swayed precariously as they walked. Theo tried to surreptitiously step between them and Simon's body in hopes that they wouldn't notice the gruesome scene, but all his movement did was draw their attention.

"Oh, I know you!" one of the woman said with a hiccup. "You're that handsome winery owner. I hear you're single? Is that true? I can hardly believe a catch like you hasn't settled down yet, but—"

The woman cut off her own sentence with a loud, bloodcurdling scream. I winced, knowing she must have just noticed Simon. Of course, as soon as she screamed, her friends started looking frantically around to see what was the matter. It only took them a few moments to notice Simon, at which point they started screaming as well. This drew the attention of tourists and locals alike, and I saw faces beginning to peek from the windows of nearby restaurants.

Theo and I looked at each other and groaned at the same time. What had been a sleepy small-town street was about to become a complete circus.

"Mitch better not have been kidding about the fact that he would get here soon," Theo muttered, just loud enough for me to hear. And then, in a much louder voice, he started addressing the gathering crowd.

"Everyone back! Everyone stand back! This is a crime scene, so unless you want your DNA all over the evidence, I suggest you stand back!"

His warning seemed to fall on deaf ears for the most part, and people continued to press forward, jostling each other for a closer look.

"Is this some sort of prank?" one confused tourist asked. "That's not really a dead man, is it?"

"I think it's one of those ghosts of Christmas past things," another very drunk tourist slurred out. "It must be some kind of production the town is putting on to try to drum up more business for their stores and restaurants. Some of these little chambers of commerce will do all sorts of gimmicky things to boost their economy."

"I dunno," said a man I recognized as one of the Sunshine Springs locals. "This seems like an odd thing for a chamber of commerce to put in the middle of the street, and I certainly haven't heard of any plans for anything like this."

"I'll just touch him and see if he's real," another tourist said, boldly taking a step forward in the direction of Simon's body. My heart tightened in my chest as I realized he was about to contaminate the crime scene! Luckily, Theo also realized the danger and was much quicker to react than I was.

"You'll do no such thing!" Theo roared, stepping between the tourist and Simon's body. He held up his hand in a "stop" motion. "This is not some sort of twisted production by the chamber of commerce. This is a crime scene. For those of you who are too inebriated to realize what you're looking at, let me explain. This is a dead body, likely the victim of a murder. If you touch him, your DNA is going to be associated with a murder scene. Is that really what you want?"

The growing crowd looked at him with a mixture of skepticism and understanding. Some people seemed to believe him, while others apparently still bought into the idea that this was some sort of joke. Luckily, before anyone else could try to step forward and touch Simon's body, Mitch arrived.

"Everyone back! Everyone back!" the sheriff bellowed as he approached the scene. He was dressed down in a hoodie and a pair of sweatpants, so he didn't look as imposing as he normally might have. But although he lacked an official police uniform, he did have his official police badge. He held it high above his head and continued to shout at the crowd to move back. Most of them were listening now, as even the last of the doubters seemed to finally understand that this was not a joke. It helped that, a few moments later, the sound of police sirens filled the air, and a few moments after that a Sunshine Springs squad car pulled up to the scene. I shuddered again as the flashing red and blue lights illuminated Simon's lifeless body. The lights also illuminated the shimmering bows that Theo and I had just hung up and down Main Street, and I frowned sadly at the sight. There was nothing like a dead body to ruin holiday cheer.

"Is it true?" a familiar voice beside me asked. "Is Simon Farrington really dead?"

I looked over in surprise to see Alice standing next to me. "What are you doing here? I wouldn't have thought you'd want to witness something like this."

Alice shifted uncomfortably from one foot to another. She'd also been tangled up in a murder case in the past, much more recently than I had. If I had been her, I probably would have been staying as far away as possible from anything that remotely resembled a homicide crime scene.

But it only took me a moment to realize that Alice's discomfort wasn't over the fact that she was standing at a crime scene. It was from the fact that she was standing there because she had been with Mitch when he received the call.

"I, just, uh…" she stammered out. "I just needed help with hanging some of the decorations at my café, so Mitch was kind enough to help out. That was very nice of him, you know. He's a nice guy. Always helping out everyone in the community. Not just me. Everyone. Anyway, he was there and I heard the call come in and I thought I should come see if I could be of any assistance."

I grinned at her in spite of the unhappy situation we were currently involved in. "Alice, it's okay if you like Mitch. You're both grownups, and if you want to spend time together, romantically or otherwise, you can. No need to feel embarrassed or explain it away. And you should know better than to try to keep any kind of relationship a secret in this town, anyway. Word gets around fast."

Alice looked simultaneously sheepish and relieved. "I just wasn't sure how you would feel about it if Mitch and I spent time together."

I put a reassuring hand on her arm. "I'm not interested in him in that way. We're good friends, but I mean it when I say that I don't want to be in a relationship of any kind right now. I'm too busy with my café, and, to be honest, I'm still too gun-shy about men after the divorce I went through."

Alice shook her head sadly. "I can't believe anyone would treat you the way your ex did. You deserve much better. You deserve someone who will take care of you. Like…Theo."

Alice's eyes lit up with mischief, and I shook a finger at her. "I'm not interested in dating Theo, either. And I don't need someone to take care of me. I can take care of myself. My pie shop is doing well, and I'm busier than ever with the holiday season in full swing. If things continue on this way, then I should have plenty of money in savings by the new year."

Alice grinned at me, the flashing police lights reflecting off her shining eyes. "Just because you don't need someone to take care of you doesn't mean you have to refuse help when it's offered. You shouldn't push Theo away so fiercely."

I opened my mouth to make some sort of retort to that, but before I could say anything, my attention was drawn back to the crime scene by the voice of Theo himself.

"Izzy! Did you see this when we first walked up? I was too focused on checking his pulse to notice, but it looks like there was definitely foul play here."

I looked over to see that Theo was pointing at something on the ground next to Simon. As I scooted over to get a closer look, Mitch glared at me.

"Don't touch anything!" he warned. He sounded exasperated, and a few moments later he cracked his knuckles loudly, telling me that he was definitely in a foul mood. He always started cracking his knuckles when he was worked up about something, but I couldn't blame him for being worked up right now. He had a crime scene to deal with, and the crowd was pressing in on his officers, trying to get a better look.

And yet, even though Mitch obviously was not in the mood for jokes, I couldn't help cracking one. "Hey," I said with a twinkle in my eye. "At least you're wearing sweats this time instead of a wrestling costume."

Mitch gave me a death glare. I was referring to another murder scene Mitch had been called to a few weeks ago, one that had occurred in the midst of the Sunshine Springs' Fall Festival costume contest. Mitch had been dressed as a wrestler at the time the murder happened, so all of the media photos of him at the scene had been of him looking a bit ridiculous in a wrestling singlet. Needless to say, it had not been his proudest moment—and it wasn't something he liked to be reminded of.

"Get away from my crime scene!" Mitch roared at me. But then he turned his attention back to the crowd pressing in on him.

Feeling only slightly guilty for getting him more riled up, I turned to see what Theo was pointing at. On the ground near Simon's motionless feet lay a sheet of paper with a message on it. But the message wasn't typed or handwritten. Instead, it was put together using letters that had been cut out of magazines and newspapers and pasted together to make words. It looked like the sort of thing I would have expected to read about in the Nancy Drew novels of my youth.

"That's wild," I murmured as I leaned in, trying to read what the note said. In the dim glow of the streetlight, making out the words was difficult. I glanced nervously back at Mitch, worried that I was about to be yelled at for contaminating evidence. But he was still busy keeping the crowd at bay. Alice had joined Theo and me by the letter as well now, and none of the police officers seemed to be paying much attention to us. I figured they were so used to seeing me at Sunshine Springs' crime scenes by now that they didn't think twice about the fact that I was there.

Mitch would think twice, however, once he got things under control enough to look back at me and realize that I was trying to investigate clues. I had to hurry if I wanted to read this note before he shooed me away for good.

Pulling my phone out of my pocket, I turned on its flashlight function and shone the light down on the paper, careful not to actually touch anything. Theo and Alice leaned over my shoulders, listening with interest as I slowly deciphered the pasted-on words.

"Hey, Cheater," I read slowly. "That's exactly what you are: a cheater. You've gone too far in your attempts to win the decorating contest, and you've forgotten the true meaning of Christmas. I know how you cheated, and I'm going to tell everyone unless you meet me in front of Moe's at 8:30 tonight. Bring one thousand dollars cash and I'll stay quiet. That's a reasonable sum for my silence, since the contest prize is five thousand dollars, wouldn't you agree? Don't be late, and don't shortchange me any of the money, or I'll tell everyone what I know."

There was, unsurprisingly, no signature on the letter. I stared at it for a few moments, then looked at the time on my phone. It was nine-fifteen, forty-five minutes now after the time that the letter had demanded Simon meet the mystery sender. I furrowed my brow, trying to remember what time, exactly, Theo and I had gone into the café.

"Were we inside already at eight-thirty?" I asked.

Theo shrugged, as unsure of an exact timeline as I was. "I don't know," he said with a shake of his head. "But it looks like we narrowly missed seeing the Grinch get poor Simon."

My blood ran cold as I remembered watching Vinny arguing with Simon right before Theo and I had gone inside. Had Vinny discovered that Simon was cheating, and taken things into his own hands to stop him? Their fight had certainly been spirited. Had Vinny's desire for a thousand dollars of blackmail money turned into a desire to just shut Simon up permanently?

"Izzy! Get back!"

I jumped, startled by the roar of Mitch's voice. He'd noticed that I was still hovering over his crime scene, and this time I had a feeling he wasn't going to get distracted and leave me alone for another few minutes. Reluctantly, Theo, Alice and I all stepped back. But just as I was stepping back, I saw a phone on the ground by Simon's feet lighting up with an incoming call. I couldn't stop myself from glancing at the caller I.D., and my heart sank in my chest when I saw that it read "Colleen."

Colleen Farrington was Simon's wife. In the midst of my shock over what had happened, and then my curiosity over trying to read the strange letter left at the crime scene, it hadn't occurred to me that Simon's family certainly didn't know what had happened, and would need to be contacted.

Officer Smith, one of Mitch's most trusted deputies, glanced uneasily over at the sheriff. "Should I answer it?"

Mitch shook his head. "Don't touch the phone. It will need to be fingerprinted. But we do need to contact Colleen. Have one of the other officers head to her home and see if they can find her to deliver the news in person."

"Um, looks like that won't be necessary," Theo said, pointing to a pair of headlights that was coming barreling down Main Street. The white sedan that the headlights belonged to was swerving wildly right and left as it sped toward the crime scene. "I'm pretty sure that white sedan belongs to Colleen."

Mitch turned to look at the speeding car, then straightened his back and got a resigned look in his eye. "This is the worst part of my job," he said softly as he started walking away from the crime scene and toward the edge of the road.

In that moment, I felt truly sorry for him. I couldn't imagine many things worse than having to inform someone that their husband had been discovered murdered.

I glanced back at Simon. Of course, the one to feel the sorriest for here was Simon. Theo was right: the Grinch had gotten to him.

But who was the Grinch? I shivered as I took a step back from Simon's body. The warm holiday feelings I'd been reveling in earlier this evening had dissipated, and a distinct chill filled the air.

Someone was trying to ruin Christmas in Sunshine Springs.

CHAPTER FOUR

"No! It can't be true! It just can't be!"

It took Mitch and two of his other able-bodied officers to hold Colleen back as she tried to launch herself toward her lifeless husband, who still hung gruesomely from the streetlamp's post, held up by the pine garland that looked entirely too cheerful for the circumstances.

"Mrs. Farrington, please," Mitch pleaded. "I understand this is upsetting, but it won't help things if you contaminate the crime scene. If we're going to find your husband's killer, we'll need to comb carefully for any DNA evidence he or she has left behind."

Colleen ignored Mitch, and I supposed I couldn't blame her. If I'd discovered that my husband had been murdered just weeks before Christmas, I probably wouldn't have listened to reason, either. Thankfully, at that moment the forensics team arrived to start collecting evidence. The sight of the official looking workers in their head-to-toe sterile blue scrubs seemed to get through to Colleen in the way that Mitch and his officers could not. She continued sobbing, but stopped fighting to get to Simon. Instead, she collapsed against Mitch's shoulder. Awkwardly, he patted her on the back, then led her to sit down on a nearby bench. When he looked up and saw that I was still standing there, I thought I was going to get yelled at again. But instead, Mitch seemed grateful to see me.

"Izzy, do you think you could get Colleen some tea or coffee from your café? Perhaps holding a warm beverage in her hand would help calm her."

I perked up at the opportunity to do something useful. "Of course."

I rushed into my café to fetch a mug of coffee, thankful that I'd already had a fresh pot of decaf brewing for Theo. Sprinkles shadowed me, as he had been since this whole debacle began. He seemed to know that a murderer might be roaming free, and he was determined to protect me from anyone sinister. He didn't even glance at the slices of pie that were still

19

sitting out on the café table untouched. I glanced at them, sighing dejectedly as I realized that Theo and I probably weren't going to be eating that pie tonight.

No matter. My problems paled in comparison to what Colleen was going through right now. And they *definitely* paled in comparison to what Simon had gone through. I shivered, and quickly poured some coffee into a takeout cup to carry out to Colleen.

When I walked back outside, she was still sitting on the bench where Mitch had placed her, sniffling and talking to Officer Smith. I approached quietly and handed the coffee over without a word, hoping that Officer Smith wouldn't notice me so that I could stand nearby and listen to what Colleen was saying.

Every time a murder case popped up in Sunshine Springs, I swore I wasn't going to get involved. But every time, I somehow got dragged into it. This time, I wasn't even going to pretend that I wasn't interested. Someone had gone too far. They had cast a shadow over what was supposed to be the happiest time of the year, and I wasn't going to let them get away with it. No matter how much Mitch or anyone else tried to deter me, I was determined to solve this case and save Christmas in Sunshine Springs.

I stood taller as these thoughts rushed through my head, ready to push back if Officer Smith tried to get me to step away from the spot where he was taking a statement from Colleen. But Officer Smith, although he was an excellent police officer, wasn't nearly as laser-focused on keeping me out of things as Mitch was. He barely looked up at me as I handed the coffee off, and then went back to talking to Colleen.

"Okay, so you were on your way to a Christmas party when you heard the news that something had happened to Simon?"

Colleen sniffled and nodded. She didn't drink from her coffee cup, but she did wrap her hands tightly around it, and I hoped that the warmth was giving her some comfort. "I was in a rush to get to the party, actually. Simon had needed my help with setting up some piece of his Christmas decorations, and so I was much later getting ready than I'd planned to be." Here, Colleen hung her head and started crying again, making it difficult to make out her words.

"There, there," Officer Smith said. "Take your time. I know this is difficult for you. Try a couple deep breaths, okay? There you go. That's the way."

Colleen managed to get in control of her emotions enough to speak, and she shook her head sadly. "I'm afraid I was rather short with Simon. I didn't want to help him with the decorations, and we had a bit of a disagreement over it. He told me I didn't care about his decorations. In fact, he went off for quite a while about how no one in town appreciated his efforts. It's not that I didn't appreciate it. It's just that I was busy getting ready for the party, and I thought he didn't respect my time. But oh! If I had known that was going to be the last time I saw him alive I would have been so much nicer. I can't believe our last words to each other were a stupid fight over tinsel."

Colleen dissolved into sobs once again, and Officer Smith was once again obliged to help calm her down. When she finally started speaking again, I saw Mitch approaching out of the corner of my eye. I knew my time to listen in was growing short, and I silently willed Colleen to hurry up and spit out what she knew. Luckily, she seemed to have reached the point that talking about it was actually helping her calm down and sort her feelings out, and the words were tumbling from her lips.

"I finally got ready, and headed to the party. It was a gift exchange for several ladies that are part of a book club I'm in. I was late, and in a rush to get there, so I didn't notice that my phone had been called several times on the drive over. It seems that word was already spreading through the grapevine that something had happened to Simon."

I glanced over at the crowd of tourists surrounding Simon, and I felt a twinge of disgusted annoyance. How could all of these people be so crass, standing around to gawk at a dead body? And how could anyone have thought it was okay to start spreading gossip about the murder before the police had even had a chance to properly notify the victim's family? I should know by now that the gossip mill in Sunshine Springs was a machine that could not be stopped, but sometimes it still took me by surprise. It must have only been a few minutes after Theo and I discovered Simon's body that the news started spreading.

"Izzy, what are you still doing here?" Mitch's voice behind me told me that my time to listen in on Colleen's statement had just about expired, but I did my best to buy myself a few more moments. I turned and flashed him a brilliant smile.

"Just making sure her coffee stays refilled," I said sweetly, then turned back toward Colleen before Mitch could reply.

"I didn't listen to any of the voicemails before I went in to the party," Colleen was saying. "I figured whatever was so important they could just tell me in person when I walked in. And of course, they did tell me. The first thing someone said when I walked in was 'Oh my god, did you hear about Simon?' They caught me up on the news pretty quickly and I drove down here as fast as I could to see if it was true…"

Colleen burst into sobs again at the same moment that Mitch grabbed my arm. "Izzy, come on. Stay out of things, okay? Someone just got strangled by a pine garland. Whoever did this is obviously a violent person, and not someone you should be tangling with."

I turned my face toward Mitch and raised an eyebrow in his direction. "I'm already pretty tangled up in this. It's hard not to be when Theo and I are the ones who found him."

"True," Theo's voice came from my other side, and I turned to see that he'd walked up to join us. "But no one is more tangled up than Simon, the poor fellow. I don't think he's ever getting out of the pine garland he got tangled up in."

I groaned and gave Theo a small punch in the arm. "I know you deal with tough situations using humor," I hissed in a low voice. "But maybe don't make jokes so loudly when Simon's newly widowed wife is sitting two feet away from you."

Theo glanced over to where Colleen sat, and he looked suitably chastised. "Oops," he whispered. "I didn't realize she was right there."

Luckily, Colleen was crying again, and her sobs were much too loud for her to have heard anything that Theo had said. Mitch had heard it all, however, and he'd clearly had enough of both Theo and me.

"Come on you two," he said, pointing toward his squad car. "It's down to the station for both of you. I need statements."

Theo, who was best friends with Mitch and had no qualms about joking around even when Mitch was in a horrible mood, put a hand over his heart in mock shock. "What? Down to the station? In a squad car? Am I under arrest? But officer, I didn't do anything, I swear!"

Theo swooned and pretended to faint, which made me giggle. Alice, who had also walked up to where we were standing, giggled as well. But one stern look from Mitch quickly silenced our giggles.

"You can ride in my car, or your car, or Izzy's car," Mitch said. "Heck, you can walk if you want. I don't care. I just want a statement from both of you tonight."

"Can I bring Sprinkles?" I asked, glancing down at my trusty Dalmatian, who was still sitting silently by my side, guarding me from whatever threats lurked in the darkness. "Otherwise I'll need to drop him off at home first. I don't want to leave him alone in the café with all this commotion going on out here."

"I'll take Sprinkles," a voice behind me called out.

I smiled as I turned. "Grams! What are you doing out here?"

My grandmother shrugged, raising the shoulders on her neon yellow cardigan. Her neon pink hair bounced slightly as she moved in to give me a hug, and I caught the sweet scent of lemon on her clothing. She must have been baking her famous lemon cake before deciding to come out to the scene of Simon's unfortunate demise, and the familiar smell brought me comfort in the midst of the rather chaotic night. My grandmother was a character, as evidenced by the fact that she always wore neon colored clothing and dyed her hair in a variety of neon shades. But despite her love of fun and frivolous fashion, she herself was anything but frivolous. She was my rock, and I hadn't realized how much I needed a rock tonight until

I saw her standing in front of me.

She must have known I needed her, though. She looked at me with searching, concerned eyes. "Rose called me and told me what happened. I imagine the whole town knows by now. Normally, I try to stay far away from these sorts of things, but when I heard that you and Theo were the ones to find Simon, I figured I should come check on you. How are you holding up?"

I sighed. "I'm alright. Just disappointed that something like this has happened. It puts a bit of a damper on the whole Christmas cheer thing, you know?"

Grams nodded sagely. "Indeed it does. I can't believe anyone would do such a thing! And so close to Christmas. Poor Colleen!"

We all glanced over at Colleen, who looked like she wasn't going to be giving much more of a statement anytime soon. She'd devolved into complete hysterics at this point, and who could blame her?

Mitch cleared his throat loudly, and pointed to his squad car again. "I'm sorry to rush you, but I really do need to get statements, and I need them tonight. I'm happy to let you ride down to the station with me, if you don't feel up to driving."

I sighed. The last thing I felt like doing right now was heading down to the police station, but Mitch didn't look like he was in the mood to take no for an answer. I glanced back at Grams. "Can you watch Sprinkles for me? I can pick him up in the morning before I open the café."

Grams nodded with a dismissive wave of her hand. "I'm happy to watch him, and no need to pick him up early in the morning. I've got an appointment at Sophia's Snips in the morning. I can take him with me and then you can pick him up in the afternoon when you're done at the café."

Sprinkles started barking excitedly at the mention of Sophia's Snips. Sophia's was the only salon and spa in town, and it was a wildly popular place for all of the women in Sunshine Springs to go. Grams was usually there at least once a week, and she loved to take Sprinkles with her. She had somehow convinced my boy Dalmatian that he needed to constantly have his nails painted, and I had given up on trying to convince him otherwise. If Grams and he both had fun, then what was the harm?

I reached down and gave Sprinkles an affectionate rub behind his ears. "Alright, boy. You can have a spa day with Grams tomorrow. I guess you've earned a chance to relax, since you're the one who alerted me to this."

Sprinkles barked with excitement, and Grams took him to her car after giving me a goodbye hug and telling me to call if I needed anything. She was concerned for my mental wellbeing, and truth be told, I was feeling a bit peeved about the whole situation. I didn't appreciate someone swooping in and causing this much trouble during my first Christmas in Sunshine

Springs.

But what right did I really have to be so upset, when Colleen had lost so much more than I had? As I looked over at her, still sobbing under the flashing lights of the police cars and the softer, twinkling Christmas lights, I determined that I was going to get to the bottom of who had killed Simon.

Whoever had done this was going to learn that you did not mess with Christmas in Sunshine Springs.

Not on my watch.

CHAPTER FIVE

The Sunshine Springs Police Station was buzzing with activity. Normally, at past nine p.m., the place would have been quiet. But tonight, every officer in Sunshine Springs had been called out to deal with the homicide crisis. Even the front desk receptionist had come in to work, although she hadn't bothered to change out of the yoga pants she'd been wearing. It was strange to see her dressed down, since she normally looked quite polished. But then, everything about this night was strange.

I sat in the lobby with Theo, watching officers rush back and forth with pale faces. Most of them were speaking in hushed tones into their cell phones, and no matter how much I strained to hear what they were saying, I couldn't quite make out the words. I grew grumpier with every passing moment, wishing that I could at least hear some inside information on the case if I had to sit here at the station for an eternity.

And it did feel as though I'd been there for an eternity. Despite Mitch's insistence that Theo and I needed to come give a statement right away, we'd been left in the lobby for almost an hour at this point, waiting for our turn to talk to the officers. Theo didn't seem bothered by this. He was scrolling through emails on his phone and occasionally cracking another joke about the Grinch being on the loose in the town. I finally gave up on trying to make him stop joking about the situation. As insensitive as his jokes might have seemed, I'd come to learn that humor was the way Theo dealt with difficult situations. He didn't mean to come across as rude. He was just trying to process the shock of everything in his own way.

At some point, Mitch must have realized that he was making us wait too long, because he sent an officer out to check on us. The officer, who was young and must have been fairly new on the force, because I didn't recognize her, opened the door to the reception area with a harried look on her face.

"Mitch asked me to tell you that it shouldn't be much longer," she said. "He's just trying to finish getting a statement from Colleen, and she hasn't been easy to calm down."

I instantly felt guilty for being so impatient. My night had been bad, but not as bad as Colleen's. "Of course. I understand. We'll be right here waiting."

The officer nodded, looking relieved at my response, and then disappeared back down the long hallway that led to the station's offices and interrogation rooms. She forgot to close the door when she left, and I stood to go stand by the open doorway, hoping I might hear something.

Theo barely looked up from his phone when I moved, but the receptionist looked up and gave me a curious stare. I smiled at her, hoping she wasn't going to feel motivated to get up and close the door. I knew Mitch wouldn't want me to eavesdrop, and she knew it, too. But I was feeling desperate for some information on what was going on. To deflect suspicion, I pulled a candy cane off of a sagging Christmas tree that stood in the corner near the hallway.

"May I?" I asked. "I could use a little jolt of sugar."

The receptionist smiled and seemed to forget about the open doorway. "Of course, Izzy. We need to get some better decorations for that tree, anyway. I know it's just a police station and we don't need anything super fancy, but those ornaments must be about fifteen years old."

I unwrapped the candy cane as I took in the simple red and green ornaments that hung from the tree's sad branches. They looked like they might have been glittery at one point, but most of the glitter had rubbed off over the last fifteen years. I was about to make a polite comment about how it wasn't really that bad, but then I bit into the candy cane and couldn't help making a face. It tasted stale, and it broke apart in brittle pieces in my mouth.

From across the room, Theo must have been watching, because he guffawed when he saw the look on my face. "That candy cane must be about fifteen years old as well."

"Theo! Don't be rude!" I said in a horrified tone, turning to look apologetically at the receptionist. I was sure she was going to march over and slam the hallway door shut in revenge. But she only sighed and shook her head sadly.

"He's probably right. I keep meaning to replace all of those decorations, but the holidays are such a busy time. I always get distracted by other things and forget."

Her cell phone buzzed loudly at that moment, and she glanced down at where it sat on the desk beside her computer's keyboard. When she saw the caller I.D., she groaned.

"Speaking of distractions, this is my mother. I better take the call. No doubt she wants to hear what I know about Simon's murder."

The receptionist answered the phone, which was a stroke of luck for me. It meant I could scoot even closer to the open doorway and try to hear what was going on in the interrogation rooms.

Unfortunately, even with the hallway door open, I couldn't make out anything that was actually being said. The door to the interrogation room where Mitch must be interviewing Colleen was closed, and they weren't speaking loudly enough for me to hear anything more than a murmur.

I looked despondently over at Theo, hoping for some sympathy, but he barely looked up from his phone as he shook his head at me. "Just sit down and eat your ancient candy cane. You'll hear all the gossip about the case tomorrow. It's going to be all anyone in town is talking about."

I made a face at him. "I'll hear all the gossip, but I won't hear any of the real evidence on the case. You know Mitch is going to be tightlipped about that. At least, you know he'll be tightlipped about it with everyone except you. Somehow you always seem to convince him to give you the inside scoop."

Theo gave me a smug grin. "What can I say? I'm just an easy guy to talk to."

"Uh-huh. It has nothing at all to do with the fact that you're his best friend?" I threw what was left of my candy cane across the room at him, and he gave me an overdramatic gasp.

"Isabelle James! You dare assault me with a candy cane right in the middle of the police station?"

I rolled my eyes at him and went to grab another candy cane from the tree, hoping that this one might magically taste better than the last one. But before I could select another one, I was distracted by the sound of Colleen's yelling coming from down the hallway.

"I'm telling you: you need to go arrest Lynette Moir. I'm sure it was her! She's been obsessed with beating Simon at the annual decorating contest, and she took that obsession too far."

I blinked in surprise and tilted my head to try to hear better. My heart pounded with excitement, and I hoped that Colleen would continue yelling so I could hear what she had to say. After a short pause, when Mitch or one of his officers must have said something, she did.

"Check the footage on our home security cameras, and you'll see what I'm talking about. She was at our house several times over the last few weeks threatening Simon. I don't know exactly what she said to him. All I know is that whatever it was made Simon quite upset."

Colleen was slowly lowering the volume of her voice, and it was getting harder for me to hear. I glanced back at the receptionist, who was quite engrossed in her phone conversation with her mother at this point. Theo was staring down at his phone again, apparently not all that interested in eavesdropping. Why would he be? Mitch would share all of this with him tomorrow, no doubt.

Me, though? If I wanted the inside scoop, I was going to have to act quickly. With one more glance to make sure the receptionist wasn't paying attention, I scooted down the hallway. I crept forward until I was standing right outside of the interrogation room where Mitch and his officers were speaking with Colleen, and from that location, I could hear Mitch as well.

"Colleen," he was saying in a soothing voice. "I will talk to Lynette, but I can't arrest her merely because she recently argued with Simon. We'd need more evidence than a few simple arguments in order to consider her a murder suspect."

Even through the closed door, I could hear Colleen sputtering. "How much more evidence do you need?" she asked in an incredulous tone. "It wasn't mere arguments. She threatened him. True, I don't know exactly what those threats were, but I know they made him upset. You saw the letter at the crime scene! She must have been accusing him of cheating, although I'm sure he wasn't doing anything of the sort. He won that contest fair and square every year. Lynette was just jealous."

Mitch sighed wearily. "I didn't realize my officers had divulged the letter's contents to you."

I almost giggled. I could just picture Mitch giving his officers an exasperated look, silently reprimanding them for telling Colleen about the letter when they knew it would only stir her up. I remembered at the last moment to stay quiet. If Mitch realized I was out here, he would certainly go through the roof with anger.

But hey, it wasn't my fault he'd insisted I come down to the station tonight. And it wasn't my fault his officer had left the door to the hallway wide open. I hadn't been strictly forbidden from being in this hallway, so who could blame me for getting up to stretch my legs when I'd been left sitting for so long?

I leaned closer to the door, nearly pressing my ear right against it, when suddenly something hit me in the back of the head. I barely managed to contain the yelp that rose up in my throat, and I winced at the sound of whatever had hit me clattering across the floor. I held my breath for a moment, thinking that surely Mitch was going to come storming out of the room to ask what was going on in the hallway, but the murmur of voices from behind the door continued. Relief flooded my being, followed a moment later by indignation. I looked down at the ground to see a cracked candy cane, then looked up to see Theo grinning at me.

"You candy-caned me first," he said, his voice sounding horribly loud to me even though he was speaking at a normal level. "Fair's fair."

"Shh," I hissed, my cheeks heating with anger. "Keep it down! And you had no right to throw a candy cane at me. It doesn't matter if I threw one first. You deserved it."

"Keep my voice down why?" Theo asked, not lowering his voice at all. "Worried Mitch is gonna realize you're out here eavesdropping?"

I rolled my eyes heavenward, and was about to make some sort of remark about how this was not the way for Theo to win me over if he really did want to date me. But before I got any words out, Colleen was screaming again. Theo and I both turned toward the door, listening with interest to her fresh tirade.

"...and what's more, the arguments aren't the only evidence I have. We also had several of the Christmas decorations in our yard vandalized a few days ago. Simon was beside himself over the incident. He worked so hard to set everything up, and then someone came through and ruined it. You should have seen it! The vandal cut off the wings of all of our lighted angel figures, and then they filled Santa's sleigh with beer bottles. They stole all of Santa's clothes so that the Santa statue was naked, and hung him upside down from the side of the sleigh to make it look like he was completely drunk. The whole thing was such a mess."

Beside me, Theo had started laughing. "Oh, man. A drunken Santa. That's rich. Do you think DWI laws apply to sleigh-flying? Or is Santa exempt as long as the reindeer aren't drunk as well?"

I glared at Theo. "It's not funny," I hissed. "It's despicable. This is not how Christmas should be, with decorations being destroyed and then a man being murdered simply because he won the contest every year."

Theo frowned. "Well, apparently it was because he cheated. At least, that's what the murderer seemed to think. But still, you're right. It's not funny. I shouldn't be laughing about it."

Theo looked like he felt suitably guilty for laughing over the matter, and, better still, he was actually being quiet. Relieved that I wasn't going to be discovered, at least not yet, I turned my attention back to eavesdropping.

"That's right!" Colleen said. "Check the security video and you'll see. Lynette was the one who destroyed the decorations. Sure, she tried to hide her identity underneath a stupid black ski mask. But she wasn't smart enough to cover her arms completely. She has that stupid tattoo of her dog's face on the inside of her wrist, and you can see it on the video. I know it was her, so don't tell me you don't have enough evidence."

Colleen burst into sobs, and I heard Mitch consulting in a low voice with his officers. I leaned right against the door to try to hear what was being said, but he was speaking too low, probably in an effort to keep Colleen from hearing him. Then, to my horror, I heard the sound of chairs scraping against the floor.

I jumped back from the door to try to make a run for the lobby, but I was too slow. A split-second later, the door to the interrogation room opened and Mitch was standing right in front of me.

His eyes widened in surprise when he saw me, then narrowed in anger. He looked up to see Theo standing there as well, and I thought we were both going to get yelled at until our eardrums burst.

But instead of yelling, Mitch looked back and forth between the two of us, and then pointed in the direction of the lobby. "Back to reception, both of you. Sit your butts in the chairs out there and don't move them until I come get you."

"I was just trying to get Izzy to come back to the lobby," Theo explained in a bright, helpful tone. I gave him a sound kick in the shin for that, and he yelped. Perhaps he'd originally been intending to get me back to the lobby, but he had been eavesdropping just as much as I had by the time Mitch caught us.

Mitch didn't seem interested in excuses, however—not even excuses from his best friend. "Out," he said, shaking his pointer finger at the lobby. "Butts in chair, both of you. Now."

Meekly, I turned to go. Theo followed along as well, looking a little less meek. This whole thing amused him, and why wouldn't it? Mitch couldn't be that angry at Theo when he always told him everything, anyway. I, on the other hand, had the feeling that I had just earned myself an extended period of time in Mitch's bad graces.

I glumly headed back to the lobby, where the receptionist was still chatting away with her mother, completely oblivious to the fact that Theo and I had ventured into the hallway, or that any drama had taken place there.

Mitch cracked his knuckles loudly, then headed back toward the interrogation room, slamming the door to the hallway shut behind him. With a sigh, I grabbed another stale candy cane from the tree and went to sit beside Theo on the lobby chairs.

It was going to be a long night.

Then again, I couldn't be too glum: I had, after all, discovered some new information on the case. I added Lynette Moir to my mental list of possible suspects, right along with Vinny Herron.

CHAPTER SIX

The night was indeed long. It had been nearly eleven o'clock before Mitch got around to taking statements from Theo and me. I couldn't be sure, but I had the feeling that he'd made us wait as long as possible to spite us for eavesdropping. I left the station in an extraordinarily grumpy mood, feeling irritated with both Mitch and Theo.

That grumpy mood wasn't improved by the early hour that my alarm clock went off. Late night or not, murder case or not, I had a café to run—a café that required me to be up early baking pies and prepping for the influx of tourists in need of a caffeine boost. Feeling like I had ten-ton weights tied around my feet, I dragged myself out of bed and down to the Drunken Pie Café.

Once I was in the café, I did start to feel a bit better. I brewed myself an extra strong pot of coffee, then fell into the familiar rhythm of baking. The caffeine woke me up and the baking soothed my nerves. As I prepped pie dough, I mulled over the events of the night before, and wondered whether today would bring any new information on what had possessed someone to kill Simon Farrington.

I wanted to track down Vinny and Lynette without delay, demanding that they tell me what they knew. But I was sure Mitch would have them down at the station first thing today, which meant I would have to bide my time for a chance to attempt a conversation with them. Besides, I had a busy day ahead of me. It was now December second, and the holiday season was only going to get busier from here on out. Wine country was abuzz with tourists who had come up from San Francisco and Silicon Valley in search of the perfect bottles for holiday entertaining and gifts. All those tourists would want to eat, and many of them would want to eat pie. It was sure to be a busy day.

Except it wasn't.

Sure, I had a rush of locals coming in when I opened, all hoping for the inside scoop on what had happened to Simon. That was unsurprising, since I was sure that by now everyone in town had heard that Theo and I had been the ones to discover the crime scene. I didn't say much to anyone beyond what I was sure they already knew. I definitely didn't tell anyone that I'd heard of the possibility that Lynette might be a suspect. That information was far too tentative, and besides, I wanted to keep everything I knew about this case to myself. The last thing I needed was everyone in town storming Vinny or Lynette before I had a chance to talk to them.

But after the locals headed off to work, the usual rush of mid-morning tourists never came. The quiet was so strange that I even went to double-check that the sign on the front door had not been accidentally left on the "Closed" side.

It hadn't. I was open for business, and I should have had a steady stream of pie-seekers at my door on this sunny December weekend morning. But the café was eerily quiet. In fact, when I went to look up and down Main Street, it was eerily quiet as well. At least, the portion of Main Street that I could see from my café was eerily quiet. I frowned as a prickle of worry took hold in my mind. Was it possible that the tourists were spooked off by the fact that I was the one who had found Simon's body? I hadn't looked at the *Sunshine Springs Gazette* this morning, but I was sure that Simon's murder, and my role in discovering it, had been front page news.

Had the tourists all read the paper and decided to stay away from my café? I felt a brief moment of panic. Surely, no one would blame me for the murder just because I had been the one to discover Simon's body! I couldn't afford to have people avoiding my café right now. Not when I was counting on a busy holiday season to help me fortify my savings and make improvements to the café.

"Quiet, isn't it?"

I turned to see Scott Hughes, Sunshine Springs' delivery man and fiancé to my best friend Molly. As usual, he held a large cardboard box as he approached my café. But his normal, signature grin was nowhere to be seen. My throat clenched up, and I instinctively knew something was wrong.

"It is quiet," I replied. "Too quiet."

I reached to open the front door of my café for him, the dread rising within me as I watched him walk in and set the box down on my front counter without cracking any of his usual jokes. After he'd set the box down, he reached up and rubbed his forehead wearily. Because he delivered packages all over town, Scott always had the latest gossip. He always shared it with me when he came by the café, and I had never wanted to hear that gossip as badly as I did right then. Something strange was going on, and I wanted to beg him to tell me what it was, but I forced myself to be quiet. It had been a while since I'd seen him so distressed, and he looked like he needed a moment to collect his thoughts before speaking.

"The tourists are all hightailing it out of town," he finally said. "That's why things are so quiet around here."

I frowned. "Why? Because of Simon's murder."

Scott nodded, and then reached into his pocket to pull out his phone. He scrolled for a few moments to find what he was looking for, then handed the phone over to me. "They're saying the place is cursed, and that anyone who visits the town before the New Year is in danger of falling victim to that curse."

"That's the most ridiculous things I've ever heard."

But Scott shrugged and pointed at the phone. "Ridiculous or not, apparently quite a few people are buying into the idea. Look."

I glanced down at his phone's screen. He had pulled up today's front page stories not from the *Sunshine Springs Gazette*, but from a big San Francisco newspaper.

"No Sunshine for Wine Country Town Plagued by Christmas Curse," I read aloud, shaking my head at the ridiculous headline. I looked up at Scott with raised eyebrows. "This can't be a serious article, can it?"

Scott sighed. "It is. Read on."

I looked back down at the phone and started scrolling through the article. The author had described Simon Farrington's murder, and then went on to say that this was the first of what was sure to be many unfortunate mishaps in Sunshine Springs over the holiday season. Allegedly, the whole town suffered from a well-known "Christmas Curse" that took numerous lives every year. No one knew where the curse had originated, but tourists were advised to take it seriously and stay away from Sunshine Springs if they valued their lives. By the time I finished the article, I was fuming.

"I can't believe anyone would believe this! I mean, a curse? People dying every year? Come on! There's not even a hint of truth to that. No one died last Christmas, right?" I crossed my arms indignantly as I looked over at Scott for confirmation.

But Scott didn't look quite so indignant. Instead, he looked thoughtful, and for a few moments I feared that he was going to tell me that there had indeed been deaths last Christmas. But after thinking for a couple of seconds, he shook his head. "No. No one died last Christmas. But the newspapers around here have been picking up on the fact that there have been a couple of high profile deaths in Sunshine Springs recently, and they're trying to continue the story by saying that those deaths were part of the curse."

I groaned. "You mean Big Al Martel? But that was a few months ago. No one can say it was because of a *Christmas* curse."

Big Al Martel, a well-known celebrity, had been killed in Sunshine Springs during the annual Fall Festival. His murder had brought the town a lot of publicity, and not in a good way.

Scott was nodding. "Yes, Big Al Martel. But not just him. They've latched onto the fact that our mayor's race a few weeks ago was tainted by murder as well. The papers are all saying that the curse started early this year, and is stronger than ever. It's all a bunch of bunk, of course, but I guess the tourists don't want to take the chance. Almost all of them left town this morning, and no one new has come in as far as I can tell."

I felt a sudden, sick sensation in the pit of my stomach. "But there isn't a curse! And we all need the tourist income to survive."

I could already see all the plans I had to build my savings and renovate the café going up in smoke. Scott didn't look happy either. Even though he didn't work directly with tourists, he still depended on them for his income. If the businesses in Sunshine Springs weren't making money, they wouldn't order supplies. And if they didn't order supplies, he wouldn't have any packages to deliver.

"It doesn't matter that there's not actually a curse," he said bitterly. "If the tourists decide there is one, we might as well be cursed. I have a wedding coming up! How are Molly and I going to get married if I'm not making any money? Neither one of us have a rich family that can pick up the tab for us."

I winced. I hadn't even thought about that. Scott and Molly hadn't set an official date for their wedding yet, but they were getting close to doing so. They'd been making grand plans for a beautiful wedding ever since they got engaged a few weeks ago, and I knew Molly would be devastated if she didn't get to have her fairytale day because a fake curse was keeping all the tourist income away from Sunshine Springs. Luckily, she worked at the local library, so her income was less dependent on the tourists. But still, if Scott's income suffered, they would be in trouble.

I put on a brave face and tried to reassure him. "Don't worry. I'm sure this will blow over. The murder is still too fresh in everyone's minds. For goodness' sake, it happened less than twenty-four hours ago. Once things settle down the tourists will come back. Besides, once the case is solved, people will see that it wasn't a curse that killed Simon. It was another human being with a vendetta against him."

I shook my head sadly, but Scott cocked his head sideways and studied me with the first hint of a smile I'd seen from him all morning. "Are you helping out on this case?"

I grinned. "Maybe. Unless Mitch asks, in which case you should tell him that no, I definitely am not investigating Simon's murder."

Scott chuckled at that. Everyone in Sunshine Springs knew how frustrated Mitch became when I tried to solve murder cases. But Scott's smile faded quickly after that. "In all seriousness, Izzy, I hope you do find the murderer soon. I'm not the only one in Sunshine Springs who can't afford a holiday season without tourists. I know you understand that."

I nodded sadly. "I understand. You haven't heard any gossip about the case, have you?"

Scott shook his head. "No, I haven't done any deliveries down at the station yet today, but I have a couple boxes to take by there later. I'll let you know if I hear anything."

"Thanks." I glanced back at the pies in my pastry case, most of which I now feared would not be sold today. "Do you want to take some pie with you? I have plenty of extra for the day, unfortunately."

Scott took some spiked Christmas pie off my hands, then headed out to make his next delivery. After he left, I went to the window and watched Main Street for quite some time. I was hoping that it had just been a slow morning, and that by the time afternoon came, the tourists would return in search of pie. But as the clock dragged past noon, I still hadn't had any customers. After a small lunch rush of locals, I decided to close down for the day. At that point, all I was doing was paying to keep the lights on for no reason. My time would be better spent sleuthing.

All day long, I'd been fretting about how my first Christmas in Sunshine Springs was ruined, but it was time to stop fretting and start doing something. I didn't care how annoyed Mitch got with me. I wasn't going to sit this case out. I was going to find out the truth behind Simon's murder and save Christmas.

CHAPTER SEVEN

After leaving the pie shop, I called Grams to see if I should go pick up Sprinkles. They were still at Sophia's Snips Salon and Spa getting their nails done, and Grams begged for more time to enjoy her spa day with her granddoggy. I tried to sound exasperated about the fact that they were still at the spa, but I couldn't help but giggle into the receiver.

"Oh, stop acting so uptight, Izzy," Grams said into the phone. "You know you love it when Sprinkles gets all spiffed up."

To be honest, I thought it was a bit ridiculous for Sprinkles to get all spiffed up. He was already spotted all over. How much spiffier did he need to be? But I did love how happy spa days with Grams made both him and her, so I always agreed to whatever spiffing up Grams wanted to do with him.

Besides, as much as I loved Sprinkles, he wasn't allowed inside my next destination, so I would have had to leave him sitting at home anyway. He'd have much more fun with Grams. Right now, I was going to pay the Sunshine Springs Public Library a visit. I knew Molly was working today, and I wanted to go check on her. I had no doubts that Scott had already talked to her about the supposed curse and how it was keeping tourists away. Molly was already a ball of stress over the wedding, so I worried that this latest development would send her into a complete panic. As her best friend and maid of honor, I felt it was my duty to check on her.

The library was quite busy, unlike my pie shop. I held back and waited a few minutes while Molly helped a few patrons check out their selection of books. I had begun to think that I was never going to get a chance to actually speak with her, when one of her junior librarians came to take over the front desk. As Molly gathered up her things, she glanced up and noticed me standing there for the first time.

"Izzy!" she smiled and waved, and I felt relieved to see that she didn't

36

look completely distraught. In fact, she looked quite happy as she gestured for me to follow her into her office.

"What are you up to?" she asked as I fell into step beside her. "You're in luck because I just finished up my shift for the day. I just need to get my things from the back and then we can hang out, if you're free."

She walked through a doorway labeled with a "Librarians Only" sign. The employees' area of the library looked exactly like you'd expect it to, with piles of books standing proudly on every available surface. I followed her into her office, which was small but decorated with care. As head librarian, she was the only employee with her own office, and I often teased her about her "cushy" job. She always responded by rolling her eyes at me and reminding me of how big my office must have been back at the law firm I'd worked at.

"I just closed down the café for the day," I said as I moved aside a pile of bridal magazines so that I could sit on the rickety guest chair in her office. "Main Street is like a ghost town."

I watched her face carefully to see how she reacted. Part of me worried that somehow Scott hadn't told her about the troubles on Main Street yet, and that I was dropping a bombshell on her. To my surprise, she waved her hand a bit dismissively.

"I heard about the curse," she said. "It's the most ridiculous thing ever. People can't possibly stay away the whole holiday season! It'll blow over in a day or two."

I raised an eyebrow at her. "I'm not so sure about that. All the local papers are pushing the story pretty hard. Even Scott is worried about this, as I'm sure you know."

"I know," she said with a groan, flopping into the chair behind her desk. "But Scott is worried about everything these days."

"To be fair, you kind of are, too," I said, then gestured to the huge pile of bridal magazines. "At least, you're worried about everything that might affect the wedding."

"I *was* worried. I've decided not to worry anymore. It's a complete waste of time."

I blinked at her in shock. I was happy to hear that she was planning to worry less, but I wasn't sure I believed her. She'd been so determined to have every detail of her wedding perfect that she'd been fretting nonstop even though they hadn't set a date yet.

She must have seen the confusion on my face, because she laughed merrily and then slid the pile of bridal magazines over into the trash. "There. You see? None of that matters."

I blinked again. "Have you lost your mind?"

"No. Quite the opposite in fact. I think I was on the verge of losing my mind. I've always dreamed of having a fairytale wedding, but after Simon's murder last night, I realized that I was focusing way too much on the things that don't matter. Life is short, and nothing is guaranteed. It sounds cliché, but it's true. Yes, I want a beautiful wedding. But the most important detail is having the perfect groom by my side. I've got that already, so the rest…" she trailed off and shrugged.

I smiled. "There's the Molly I know."

"I guess I had gone a bit crazy, huh? Nothing like someone getting murdered in your town to bring you back down to earth."

"Or to bring your business crashing down around you," I said drily. "As much as I wish I could share your optimism, it looks like my plans for grand holiday sales are officially in the toilet."

Molly's happy face did take on a tinge of concern. "You really think so? People can't possibly believe all that rubbish, can they?"

"They believed it today. If they believe it tomorrow, and the day after and the day after…it could turn into a horrible Christmas for Sunshine Springs."

Molly narrowed her eyes at me. "Okay, I know you pretty well, and something about that glint in your eyes tells me that you have a plan on breaking this so-called curse."

I shrugged sheepishly. "You do know me well. And you can probably guess what my plan is, but I'll tell you anyway: I'm going to figure out who murdered Simon. I'm sure there's an explanation for it that doesn't involve a curse."

"And how does Mitch feel about this plan?"

I winked at her. "What he doesn't know can't hurt him. You wanna help me?"

Molly laughed. "Why not? It's been a while since I've done some good sleuthing with you. What's your plan?"

I quickly explained to her what I'd overheard at the station the night before. "I think we should go pay Lynette a visit."

Molly frowned doubtfully. "You think she'll talk to us if we just walk up to her house and ring the doorbell?"

"Maybe, maybe not. But we've had some pretty good luck in the past by just winging it like that. It's worth a shot."

Molly considered this. "True. And what's the worst that could happen? She kicks us off her property and tells us never to come back?"

I groaned. "Molly, how many times do I have to tell you? We probably shouldn't be asking what's the worst that could happen when dealing with a potential murderer."

Molly giggled. "True enough. Well, anyway. You're right. It is worth a shot. We might as well go now, huh?"

I nodded. "The sooner the better. I'm sure as time goes by and the search for Simon's murderer ramps up, Lynette is only going to grow more reluctant to talk."

I stood to leave, but Molly held up a hand. "Wait! Before we go, it's selfie time."

"You want to take a selfie right now? Whatever for?"

I wasn't all that surprised by the request. Molly was obsessed with taking selfies, and was always finding the most random reasons to indulge in one. But she must have taken plenty of selfies in her library office over the years. Why would she suddenly need another one now?

She pointed down at the trash can. "We need those bridal magazines in the background. Come here and crouch a little bit so we can get the angle right."

I let out a small sigh, but did as she asked. We both crouched at the most awkward angle possible so that Molly could manage to get our heads and the trash can full of bridal magazines all in one shot. Once she was satisfied with the selfie, she paused to upload it to her social media account. I waited patiently, having long given up on trying to convince her that she didn't need to keep her photo albums quite so updated. It made her happy, so what was the harm?

After a moment of typing, she triumphantly pushed the phone into my face. "There! It's a cute one, wouldn't you agree?"

I looked at the phone with mild interest, but then smiled. She was right. It was a cute one, and the caption she'd put alongside the photo warmed my heart:

No need for these bridal magazines to tell me how to have the perfect wedding. My maid of honor/best friend is all the support I need. Lucky to have her.

I gave Molly a quick hug. "And I'm lucky to have you. Now, let's go catch a murderer."

Molly grinned as she grabbed her purse and slung it over her shoulder. "Let's."

CHAPTER EIGHT

"This feels like just like old times," Molly said, looking over at me with a wide grin.

I had to laugh. "Is it weird that a good portion of our friendship has been spent in my car, chasing down murderers?"

Molly shook a finger at me. "Not weird. Awesome. You don't even realize how amazing you are."

I rolled my eyes at her compliment, but in truth, I was pleased. All of my friends had, at one time or another, questioned whether my affinity for detective work was a wise life choice—and Molly was no exception to that. It felt good when she acknowledged that I was skilled at chasing down criminals, and my chest puffed up a bit with pride despite my efforts to appear humble.

Right now, Molly and I were sitting in my parked car a few houses down from Lynette Moir's house. We were trying to decide whether we should indeed go knock on her door and request to speak to her, or whether it might be smarter to try to stalk her a bit and see what she was up to without telling her we were onto her. If we were careful, we could eavesdrop on some of her conversations, and perhaps learn more about what she had been up to in the last several weeks. I couldn't shake the possibility that perhaps knowing who she hung out with and what she'd been doing might lead us to more clues about how she was connected to Simon Farrington.

Molly and I debated back and forth about this for a good ten minutes, until we were interrupted by a sharp rap on my window. Startled, I let out a little yelp and looked over to see who was responsible. I found myself staring face-to-face with Lynette Moir.

"Looks like our decision on whether to talk to her was just made for us," Molly observed in a wry tone.

With a sigh, I rolled down my window and gave Lynette an innocent smile. "Hello, Lynette. How are you doing?"

Lynette snorted at me. "I'm doing about as well as could be expected, considering I spent much of my morning at the police station trying to explain that I had nothing to do with Simon's demise. I can't say I'm sorry to see him go, but I can say I had nothing to do with it. There was no love lost between us, but I wouldn't have killed him. I certainly wouldn't risk spending life in prison over the likes of *him*."

She huffed, and shook her head as though she were tossing her hair over her shoulder. The movement lost a bit of its effect since her bottle-blonde hair was cut into a short, sleek bob, and there wasn't enough of it to actually toss. As I looked her up and down, I saw that her hair wasn't the only part of her that she'd enhanced. Her face clearly bore quite a bit of makeup, and although she must have been somewhere around fifty years of age, she had an affinity for glitter eye shadow that would have rivaled any of the teens down at the high school. Her nails also sparkled. They had been painted with bright red nail polish overlaid with silver glitter. Her clothes were just as flashy as the rest of her. She wore a bright red skirt suit with leopard print trim on the collar. She tottered on sky-high red heels that were the complete opposite of sensible, and she peered at me over cat's eye glasses encrusted with rhinestones.

I blinked, unsure of what to say to her. I had seen her around town now and then, but only from afar. She was a sight to behold, and the shock of seeing her right next to my car, along with the shock of simply seeing what she actually looked like up close, left me speechless.

"I...I...uh..."

Luckily, Molly jumped in and saved me. "That sounds like an upsetting day, Lynette! But perhaps you'll feel better knowing that we think your Christmas decorations are superb. We were just in the neighborhood and decided to drive by to check them out, since we know you always have one of the best displays in Sunshine Springs."

I breathed a small sigh of relief. That was a perfectly reasonable explanation for what we were doing here, wasn't it? But one look at Lynette's face told me she wasn't buying it. She snorted again, and rolled her eyes at me.

"I wasn't born yesterday, dearies, although sometimes I try to make myself look like I was with all the Botox I've had injected into my face."

I blinked again.

Lynette laughed. "Really, Izzy, you're a bright girl, so it surprises me that you think you could come by my house and act like it's not related to Simon's murder. I know you like to play detective on these cases, and I'm sure this case is no different. You're here to try to get the inside scoop on me, are you not?"

"I, uh...I really just wanted to see your decorations," I said weakly.

Lynette shook her head at me. "You're not fooling me. But since you're here, you might as well come in."

"Come in?" I repeated, confused.

"Yes. Come in. To my house. You want to talk to me, don't you? Well then, come talk. I'll brew you some Christmas tea and you can ask me whatever silly questions you want about Simon."

She turned on her heel and started heading down the sidewalk toward her house. I turned to look at Molly.

"Did that really just happen? Lynette Moir is inviting me in for tea even though she knows I suspect her in Simon's murder?"

Molly shrugged. "Stranger things have happened. Maybe she's innocent and isn't afraid of you. Or maybe she's guilty and wants to trick you into thinking she's innocent."

"Huh. Should we go?"

"Laaaaaaaaadies!" Lynette's voice came floating through my still-open window. "I'm waaaaaaiting."

"We should go," Molly said. "We came here to talk to her, didn't we?"

"You think it's safe?"

"I don't think she's going to murder both of us in her own house, if that's what you're asking. That would be a bit tough to hide or explain away."

"True," I said slowly. "And I am quite curious to see what she has to say. She seems like quite a character."

I rolled my window up and Molly and I followed Lynette into her home, where my observation that she was a character was definitely confirmed. It wasn't just her yard that was filled to the max with Christmas decorations. The inside of her home also had Christmas paraphernalia stuffed into every possible nook and cranny—most of it sparkly. The few decorations that weren't seasonal were leopard or zebra print, and I couldn't resist a glance at Molly to see if she was as amused by all of this as I was. From the glint in her eyes, I guessed that she was.

Apparently, I wasn't as surreptitious in my observations as I'd tried to be, because Lynette noticed my fascination with her décor.

"Yes, yes, I know," she said, as though answering a question no one had actually asked. "I do like things to be glitzy, and I am quite partial to animal prints. A little touch of leopard spots here and there just makes everything so glamorous, don't you think?"

"Um, yes. Of course," I said, trying to sound sincere. I didn't necessarily hate glitter or animal prints, but I wasn't used to having it quite as in-my-face as it was inside Lynette's house.

Thankfully, Lynette seemed satisfied with my answer. She motioned to Molly and I to sit, and then went to brew tea for us. Molly sat in silence as we waited at her dining room table. I didn't dare try to whisper anything to

Molly for fear that Lynette would overhear. The flashy woman seemed to have eagle ears, and I had a feeling that no matter how low I kept my voice, Lynette would be able to hear what I was saying.

Thankfully, we didn't have to wait in silence for very long. Lynette quickly brewed tea and arranged an assortment of scones on a silver tray, which she proudly placed in front of us.

"They're Christmas scones. My own recipe," she said proudly. "I make at least a batch of them every day during the holiday season. I'm practically famous for them among my circle of friends."

I realized then that I wasn't sure who was actually in Lynette's circle of friends. Sunshine Springs was a small town, but I was relatively new here, so I was still working out which groups everyone "belonged" in. If someone hadn't crossed paths with me or my Grams on a regular basis, then I often didn't know that much about them.

I looked down at the pile of scones in front of me, and for a brief moment, I wondered whether I should worry that Lynette had poisoned them. I felt guilty for even thinking that when she was being so hospitable to us, but could anyone really blame me for having the thought? She was a murder suspect, after all. Who knew what kind of shenanigans she might pull. I chewed my lower lip as she poured some tea into my teacup and then into Molly's. Was the tea safe to drink? I glanced over at Molly, wondering if she was having similar thoughts.

If she was, she didn't let that slow her down. Molly gave me a slight shrug, then took a sip of tea before grabbing one of the scones and biting into it.

"Mmm. This is delicious. No wonder you're famous for them." Molly gave me an encouraging smile, and I decided I would have to sample the scones as well. At least Molly hadn't fallen over dead in an instant, so if there was poison in there it wasn't that strong. I lifted a scone to take a tentative bite, and relaxed a bit when I saw that Lynette was also raising a scone to her lips. Surely, she wouldn't be eating one if she'd poisoned them. Lynette also took a sip of tea, which had come from the same teapot from which she'd poured my tea, and I relaxed even more. Lynette wouldn't be eating and drinking with us if she'd poisoned our food and drink. I was letting my overactive imagination get away with me.

Never one to turn down a good scone, as long as I knew it wasn't poisoned, I happily took a generous bite of the scone I held in my hand. As soon as the rich flavors hit my tongue, I couldn't hold back a moan. The smooth, buttery flavor had a slightly cranberry-orange hint to it, and it was perfectly sweet without being overpoweringly sugary. For a moment, I forgot to be wary of Lynette.

"My goodness!" I exclaimed. "This might be the most delicious Christmas scone I've ever tasted. No wonder your friends ask you to bake them constantly!"

Lynette's face beamed with pleasure. "It's an old family recipe that I tweaked, and now it's perfect, if I do say so myself. These scones are the highlight of my holiday season every year."

I sipped my tea, which was a strong black tea with hints of orange that complemented the scones quite well. For a few moments, I forgot that I was at the house of a potential murderer to investigate her involvement in a horrible strangling. Instead, I breathed in deeply of the scents of freshly baked scones and richly brewed tea, and imagined that I was at a proper Christmas tea party.

My moment of reverie was cut abruptly short by Lynette's decision to take off her bright red leopard print blazer.

"It's warm in here," she mused as she fanned herself with a napkin. "Especially after a few sips of hot tea."

But my thoughts weren't on the temperature of the room. Instead, they were on the tattoo on Lynette's arm—a black and white drawing of what looked like a Bichon Frise, if my knowledge of dog breeds served me right. The tattoo was on the inside of her wrist, and had been fully covered by the long sleeves of her blazer. But now, Lynette was wearing only a simple sleeveless blouse, and the unique tattoo was fully visible. Seeing it reminded me of Colleen's claim that she had seen the tattoo on her home's security camera, and therefore knew that Lynette had been the one to destroy Simon's decorations.

I remembered then why I was actually here in Lynette's house. I wasn't supposed to be indulging in scones. I was supposed to be grilling Lynette to see if I could get any information out of her that might explain what had happened to Simon. I gulped down the bite of scone in my mouth, and tried to figure out which question to ask first.

Lynette, however, spoke up before I had a chance to. Ever the observant one, she noticed that I was staring at her tattoo, and chuckled. "It's an unusual tattoo, isn't it? People are always surprised that I have it. I guess they don't expect a woman in her fifties who has an affinity for sparkles and animal print to also be tattooed. But what can I say? I'm full of surprises."

She laughed and took another sip of her tea. Meanwhile, I looked over at Molly, who was raising her eyebrow at me ever so slightly. I knew she was probably wondering, as I was, whether one of the surprises Lynette was full of was that she was a cold-blooded murderer. I shivered, but kept up a calm demeanor as best I could. It had been a stroke of luck that Lynette had been so willing to invite me inside. I didn't want to give her a reason to change her mind and kick me out before I had a chance to ask her some questions about Simon.

"It's a lovely tattoo," I said, trying to sound sincere. I wasn't totally lying. The drawing of the dog was quite detailed, and had obviously been done by someone very talented. "I understand that's a picture of your dog?"

"Yes, that's Fluffy. Isn't she darling? Maybe you'll get to meet her before you leave. She's terribly shy, so she always hides in the kitchen when people first come over. But if they stay a while, her curiosity usually gets the best of her and she comes out to say hello."

When Lynette told me her dog's name, I again felt surprised. I would have expected someone as eccentric as Lynette to come up with a bit more unique of a name, but of course I said nothing. Lynette seemed like the sort of person who couldn't be put into a box.

But was she the sort of person who would take someone's life? If I was going to make any progress on this case, I was going to have to ask her questions about more than just scones and fluffy white dogs. Taking a deep breath, I decided that the best course of action was to just dive right in with my questions.

"I'm sorry you had such a horrible morning down at the police station," I said, trying to sound as sincere as I could. "But it sounds like your Christmas has already been a bit stressful. I've heard folks saying that you and Simon were arguing about the decorations in his yard. Mitch must have talked to you about that?"

I left my question purposely vague, hoping that she would angrily start ranting when I mentioned Simon. I wasn't disappointed. Her eyes darkened, and for a moment I feared that she was actually going to throw her teacup across the room. In the end, she settled for setting the cup down a little too hard, causing a loud clanging sound as it hit the saucer. I jumped a bit at the noise, but Lynette didn't notice. Instead, she got a bit of a far-off look in her angry eyes, as though remembering something from a long time ago. It took her a moment to finally begin speaking, but once she did, she barely stopped to take a breath.

"Yes, Simon and I argued about the decorations in his yard. I felt that his decorations were always too over-the-top, and I made no secret of that fact."

I nearly spit out my tea. "Over the top?" If anyone was over-the-top, Lynette was the guilty party. But apparently she didn't see things that way.

"Yes. He made heavy use of lights, and not just colorful lights that cast a warm, festive glow. Oh, no. Simon had to have the brightest, flashiest lights. His yard was covered in them. It looked more like some sort of twisted Christmas nightclub than a tasteful holiday display. Strictly speaking, the lights aren't against the rules of the decorating competition. But they were just so garish. It's such a cheap party trick to just put up a big light show instead of putting actual thought into your decorations."

Lynette shook her head sadly, as though humanity itself had no hope left, as evidenced by the garishness of the late Simon Farrington's

Christmas display.

I looked at Molly, and immediately regretted it. As soon as I saw the look in her eye, I found it nearly impossible to hold back the laughter that was trying to bubble up in my throat. Lynette didn't have much room to talk about garishness, if you asked me. Not when her own yard was about ninety-nine percent covered with glitter. Luckily, Lynette was too wrapped up in her rant to notice my amusement.

"I'm not the only one who thought his decorations were over the top," she continued. "If you ask me, it's no surprise he ended up strangled. The only thing more obnoxious than his decorations were the words that came out of his mouth. He was constantly bragging about how his decorating capabilities were so far beyond what anyone else in Sunshine Springs could do. Can you believe it? The nerve to say such a thing, when his only real decorating capabilities were that he knew how to swipe his credit card to buy more and more lights every year."

Lynette let out a disgusted huff, and I resisted the urge to point out that he *had* won the decorating contest every year, so the judges must have also thought that his decorating capabilities were excellent. Instead, I pushed for more information on what I was really interested in.

"Who else thought he was obnoxious?" I asked. Translation: who else might have had a reason to kill him?

Lynette didn't miss a beat. "Oh, lots of people. I'm pretty sure his own wife thought his decorations were obnoxious, although of course she would never have admitted that to me."

I frowned. Colleen had sounded a bit exasperated about the fact that she'd had to help Simon fix his decorations before going to her Christmas party the night before. But knowing that a husband and wife disagreed on Christmas decorations wasn't exactly earth-shattering news. Didn't every couple disagree on the best way to decorate, to some extent? And Colleen clearly wasn't the murderer. She hadn't been anywhere near Main Street when Simon died, and Mitch had already questioned her thoroughly. I wasn't interested in the petty lovers' quarrels she'd had with Simon. No, what I needed was information on who had had a big enough beef with Simon to actually want to strangle him over that beef. I desperately wanted to ask Lynette whether she knew anything about Vinny, but I was determined not to put words in her mouth. I didn't want to suggest any suspects to her, which might subtly influence what information she told me. Instead, I wanted her to tell me what she knew without prompting.

To my relief, her next rant involved Vinny, without any prompting from me.

"If you want to know who truly hated Simon, you should go talk to Vinny!"

My heart pounded in my chest with excitement, but I forced myself to keep my voice calm. "Oh?"

"Yes, Vinny," Lynette repeated, nodding her head emphatically. "He and Simon went after it like cats and dogs nearly every day. As I'm sure you know, Vinny is quite the environmentalist."

"I know," I said with a wince, thinking back to how belligerent Vinny had been the night of Simon's death.

Lynette must have mistaken the reason for my wince, because she shook a finger in my direction. "Now, now. I don't have any problem with taking care of the environment. I think we should take care of our Mother Earth. She's the only home we've got, after all. But I don't agree with Vinny's methods at all. Yelling at people and vandalizing their property is no way to convince them to join your cause. Vinny needs a lesson on sweetening his message."

I wanted to comment that Lynette herself had supposedly been caught on camera vandalizing Simon's property, but I held my tongue. I didn't want to make her defensive when she was on the cusp of telling me more about Vinny.

"I tell you what," Lynette said, shaking her finger at Molly and me for emphasis. "This rage Vinny has over Christmas decorations is nothing new. Every year he goes around and tells people that killing pine trees and putting up plastic decorations is actually ruining Christmas. But this year he's really ramped up his efforts. I don't know what bee he got in his bonnet, but he's been downright unbearable. He's been picketing outside the Christmas tree farm that old Stuart runs, even though Stuart pays to have two new trees planted for every tree he sells!"

Lynette paused to take a sip of her tea, shaking her head again as though humanity itself could not be helped. I finally couldn't help giving her just a little nudge to see if she thought that Vinny might have been the one to kill Simon.

"But do you think Vinny was angry enough to actually strangle Simon?" I asked. "That seems a bit over the top, even for someone as infamous for going too far as Vinny is."

Lynette shrugged. "A year ago, I would have agreed. But Vinny has gone so crazy this year that I can't help but think that maybe he just got caught up in his fervor for the environment and took it out on Simon before truly thinking through what he was doing. If I had to put money on who murdered Simon, my money would be on Vinny. Truth be told, though, I'm quite disappointed that things turned out the way they did. I'm not sorry to see Simon go, but I am sorry that he went before I could beat him at the Christmas decorating competition. And I'm quite sure I would have beaten him this year."

I heard Molly choke on a bite of her scone, and I nearly choked on the sip of tea I'd just taken. I couldn't quite contain the shock of hearing

Lynette so brazenly say that she wasn't sorry Simon was dead. How could anyone be so insensitive?

Lynette didn't notice our shock, however, and she leaned back in her chair as she continued on in a voice that now sounded downright wistful. "Yes, this would have been my year. I saw a great opportunity to exploit the feud between Simon and Vinny. Simon was so flustered by Vinny that he was making mistakes in his decorating. He even wired an entire half of the lights on his house all wrong, and had to spend a whole day fixing it." Lynette chuckled merrily at Simon's misfortune, and took a bite of scone before continuing. "Not to mention, Simon had to deal with Vinny bugging him on a daily basis. Vinny would go over there and yell at Simon that the plastic it took to make all of those light strings was killing all the fish in the ocean."

I frowned as I listened to all of this. "Not to sound too self-righteous, because I'm certainly not perfect when it comes to taking care of the environment, but if Vinny was upset about Simon's decorations, why wasn't he upset about yours, too? Your glittery, plastic figurines can't be all that much better than Simon's strings of lights, can they?"

Lynette sat up proudly and shook her head. "My decorations all use eco-friendly glitter this year. Not only that, but I made a donation to Vinny's favorite ocean cleanup fund, and made sure he knew about it. He still isn't thrilled with me, but those two things were enough to keep him off my back. I was hoping that with Vinny constantly bothering Simon instead of me, that I'd be able to gain some sort of upper hand in the decorating contest. I thought the distraction would hold Simon back just enough for me to finally win. I never thought Vinny would actually get angry enough to kill Simon!"

"And you do think that's what happened?" Molly asked. "You really think that Vinny is the one who strangled Simon?"

Lynette nodded. "Most definitely. Call it a crime of passion, I suppose. Vinny was so passionate about the environment that he went a bit crazy and took Simon out. Which is bad news for me, because now, even if I win the decorating contest this year, I didn't technically beat Simon. I'll never beat him now, since the old fool went and got himself murdered before I could."

Lynette slammed her teacup down again, and I jumped, unsure of what to say. What *did* one say when a murder suspect seems to only care about the fact that they can't best the murder victim in a decorating contest? Lynette was not shy about emphasizing and reemphasizing the fact that she was delighted that Simon was gone. Her only regret seemed to be that he hadn't waited a few more weeks to go, so that she could have sent him to the afterlife with the knowledge that he'd been defeated in the Sunshine Springs Christmas Decorating Contest.

I looked over at Molly, who raised her shoulders in a barely perceptible shrug. She wasn't sure what to say to Lynette either. I decided to ask Lynette about the vandalizing of Simon's decorations in one last attempt at getting information from her. At this point, I was tired of playing nice and dancing in circles around the issues, so I got straight to the point.

"Colleen says she has you on her security cameras destroying Simon's decorations."

Lynette rolled her eyes. "So I hear. Mitch asked me about that, too. I don't know what Colleen thinks she sees on those videos, but I can tell you it's not me. I wouldn't stoop as low as destroying another competitor's decorations. Not only am I too much of a lady to act in such a disgraceful manner, but if you get caught sabotaging another competitor's yard, then you're banned from the competition for life."

"For life?" Molly asked in a shocked voice. I choked, biting my tongue to keep from making a snide remark about how I wasn't so sure that Lynette fit my definition of a proper lady.

But Lynette merely nodded as she calmly reached to pour herself more tea. "Yes, for life. There were quite a few problems with that sort of thing several years ago, so the committee in charge of the contest decided to make the consequences for foul play quite severe. I don't know of any of the other participants who would risk a lifetime ban from the competition. But Vinny? He wouldn't care. He's not interested in competing, so being banned from the competition wouldn't matter to him."

I rolled this information over in my mind, making a note to check on the rules of the decorating competition and see if Lynette was telling the truth. True, it'd be odd for her to lie about something that I could so easily check into, but I was having trouble believing that a lifetime ban on a competition was a real thing. That seemed rather extreme. I also didn't know how Colleen could have possibly mistaken Lynette's tattoo on the security camera footage.

I glanced over at the tattoo again, trying not to be obvious about the fact that I was studying it. Luckily, Lynette was busy choosing another scone for herself, and didn't notice my staring. The tattoo was quite elaborate, and the odds of someone else in Sunshine Springs having a tattoo even remotely similar were quite low. It wasn't the sort of tattoo you'd accidentally mistake for another lookalike tattoo. Either Colleen was completely lying about the video footage, or Lynette was completely lying about not being the vandal. I couldn't see what reason Colleen would have to lie, and I was starting to suspect that Lynette was telling a bunch of lies just to get Molly and me off her back. The strategy wouldn't work long-term, since the information she was lying about was so easily verifiable. But maybe Lynette didn't care. Maybe she just wanted to get us out of her hair for the time being at least.

If that was the case, Molly and I might as well leave. We were just wasting our time listening to Lynette's wild fibs, and I needed to go pick up Sprinkles. I had just opened my mouth to make an excuse for why I needed to get going when a white ball of fur rushed into the room and started barking at me. I looked down to see a dog that exactly matched the tattoo on Lynette's arm. It was wearing a sparkly rhinestone collar and leopard print booties, and it was not happy to see me.

"Fluffy!" Lynette cried out. "Fluffy, down! Stop being rude to our guests."

Lynette started making hurried apologies for Fluffy's behavior, saying that the dog didn't usually act that way and must be stressed out over the events of the last day. I stood, and waved away Lynette's apologies.

"It's alright. I need to get going, anyway, and I don't want to stress Fluffy out any more than she already is."

Molly, looking relieved, stood and practically ran to the door as she called out a quick thank you for the scones over her shoulder. I was forced to hurry if I wanted to leave the house at the same time as her, so I made an exit that was almost as quick. Lynette didn't try to slow us down, and Fluffy didn't stop barking even after the front door closed behind us. I could still hear the determined little furball growling and yipping as we walked down the path through the front yard.

"Jeez, Molly, could you have hightailed it out of there any faster?" I asked, huffing slightly as I tried to keep pace with her.

Molly shook her head. "Sorry. I'd just had enough, and that dog gave me the creeps. She had this look in her eye like she could see into my soul or something."

I gave Molly an incredulous look. "Are you serious? You think a dog can see into your soul? Since when have you been superstitious like that?"

Molly slowed as we reached the sidewalk. "I know it sounds crazy. I just didn't like the dog. Maybe it's because it looks exactly like that tattoo on Lynette's arm. The whole experience was just weird, and I got a really weird vibe from Lynette."

I sighed. "I did, too, but I don't feel like I got any really good information from her. She seemed more like she wanted to tell us whatever we needed to hear to leave her alone."

"Bingo," Molly said. "Which makes her seem a bit guilty, don't you think?"

"It definitely gives me pause." I frowned. "But don't you think it's strange that she denies vandalizing Simon's decorations, even though Colleen supposedly has it on video? Why would she lie about something that Colleen has proof of?"

Molly shook her head. "I don't know. Are you sure Colleen has the video footage she says she does?"

"I guess I'm not. I'll have to find a way to get the information out of Mitch. Maybe Theo will tell me. I'm sure Mitch has told him all about the case."

Molly nodded, but then fell silent. When we reached my car, I climbed in and started the engine, but didn't put the car in drive for a few moments.

"What are you thinking?" Molly asked.

I shrugged. "I was just thinking that Lynette doesn't seem strong enough to strangle someone like Simon. He was a big guy. Vinny seems like he would have been much more capable of pulling off the murder. But then why was Lynette fighting with Simon and vandalizing his property?"

"Maybe the two things aren't related," Molly suggested. "Lynette might have been fighting with Simon because they were so competitive about the decorating contest, but just because there was bad blood between them, that doesn't necessarily mean she killed him. The two incidents are probably unrelated, and she just feels compelled to deny everything because she knows that fighting with him and vandalizing his property makes her look suspicious in the murder case."

"You might be right," I said as I finally started driving forward. "And Vinny was fighting with Simon constantly as well. He seems much more likely to have ended his fights with a murder than Lynette does."

"But her dog still gives me the creeps," Molly insisted.

I laughed. "Fluffy does have crazy eyes. I'll give you that. Speaking of dogs, I need to go get Sprinkles from Grams' house. Do you want to come with me, or should I drop you off back at the library first."

"I'll come with you," Molly said. "Scott's busy tonight, so I don't have anything much to do. And odds are good your Grams will have some good holiday baking to share with us."

I laughed at the twinkle in Molly's eyes. "Odds are good indeed. She does usually have something freshly baked during the holiday season, although I'm not sure I can stuff down another bite after those scones. Lynette may be a bit strange, but I have to admit that her scones are delicious."

Out of the corner of my eye, I could see Molly shaking her head. "The scones were good but they were nowhere near as good as what your Grams bakes. I always have room for her goodies. It's easy to see where you get your baking talent from."

I smiled at Molly's praise, then turned the car in the direction of Grams' house. I would be shocked if she didn't have something freshly baked for us to sample, but it wasn't the baked goods I was most interested in. I was interested in knowing whether Grams had heard any gossip at Sophia's Snips earlier in the day. I knew she'd taken Sprinkles with her for a spa day, and there was nowhere better in Sunshine Springs to hear gossip than at Sophia's Snips. It was possible Grams had heard updates on the case that I hadn't heard yet.

I was hoping she had, because I felt like I'd made absolutely no progress during my visit to Lynette's house. There were indications that both Lynette and Vinny disliked Simon, but without more than a few arguments, I didn't have any solid evidence that either of them had committed murder.

I needed something more, and I was hoping that Grams had heard something more.

CHAPTER NINE

When I pulled onto Grams' street, I was surprised to find that nearly every spare inch of curb space already had a car parked next to it. The whole street was filled with vehicles, and I finally settled for parking right behind Grams' car in her driveway. I was blocking her in, but I figured I'd move if I needed to. It didn't look like she was planning on going anywhere anytime soon.

It looked like she was having a giant party.

"I think you'll find plenty of baked goods inside," I said to Molly as I climbed out of my car and was greeted by the sound of loud, peppy Christmas music spilling out from Grams' front door.

Molly's eyes widened as she took in the sparkling red Christmas bows that hung over Grams' front door. "You didn't tell me she was having a Christmas party."

"Because I didn't know she was having one. Come on. Let's go see if poor Sprinkles is surviving all the hullabaloo." I pushed the door open without bothering to ring the doorbell. No one would have heard it over the din, anyway.

Poor Sprinkles, it turned out, was having a grand time. I saw him almost immediately, sitting in Grams' living room surrounded by a group of Grams' friends who were drinking champagne and feasting from plates piled high with treats. They were sharing generous morsels of those treats with Sprinkles, and I saw his tail swinging back and forth at top speed. No doubt, he was completely hyped up on sugar. I sighed as I watched him, hoping he wasn't going to have a stomachache later. One thing was certain: he and I were both going to need a sugar detox come January.

But I'd worry about that in January. I swiped a peppermint macaroon from a tray on an end table before making my way toward the kitchen. Sprinkles hadn't noticed me, and I figured I'd let him continue enjoying the party for a few more minutes before putting the kibosh on his sugar hunt. I smiled at the festive red and green bandana tied around his neck, and then rolled my eyes when I noticed that his toenails were painted bright red and green. Looks like he and Grams had thoroughly enjoyed their spa day.

Molly followed me into the kitchen, also stuffing macaroons into her mouth. But macaroons were far from the only treats available. On the large countertops in Grams' kitchen sat every type of holiday treat imaginable. There were Christmas cakes, Christmas cookies, Christmas scones, Christmas trifle, Christmas pudding, Christmas pie, Christmas brownies…and the list went on. A large bowl of Christmas punch sat on the center of her kitchenette table, along with several bottles of champagne. Several more ladies were in the kitchen, also holding glasses of champagne and munching on the abundance of goodies. Grams had her back to me when I walked in, but a few moments later she turned around and her eyes lit up like the lights on a Christmas tree when she saw me.

"Izzy! What a fabulous surprise!"

I crinkled my nose in amusement. "I told you I was coming over to pick up Sprinkles. Did you forget?"

Grams furrowed her brow. "Oh, right. I suppose I did forget. I've been having so much fun that it must have slipped my mind that he was leaving soon."

She looked disappointed, and Molly laughed. "Better not tell him that he's leaving soon. He's having a grand old time mooching treats off of everyone in the living room."

Grams grinned and shrugged, clearly not willing to take any responsibility for the fact that her granddoggy was currently on the mother of all sugar highs. I should have been mad, but I could never quite manage to be mad at Grams. She was my favorite person in the world, and I admired the way she fully embraced life. She had more spirit than most women half her age.

Right now, it looked like she'd embraced the Christmas spirit fully. Her hair, which was normally a varying shade of neon, had been dyed half-red and half-green. Her nails were painted in alternating red and green, just like Sprinkles' nails, and instead of her usual neon-colored outfit, she wore a bright red dress and layers upon layers of green beaded necklaces. In some ways, she was just as eccentric, if not more, than Lynette Moir. But Grams pulled off that eccentricity much better—probably because she smiled more and had a much warmer personality.

"You like the change?" Grams' asked, noticing that I'd been eyeing her hair and nails. "I'll be back to neon come January, but I figured it'd be fun to get into the holiday spirit with the red and green."

"Looks like you also got into the holiday spirit with baking. Have you been baking all day?" I looked over the piles of treats, then helped myself to a brownie before heading toward the champagne bottles. After a day like the one I'd had, a glass of cool bubbles sounded divine.

"I suppose I have," Grams said, waving a spatula over her head. "I spent the morning at the spa with Sprinkles, then came home and felt like doing a little bit of baking."

"A little bit?" Molly said with a laugh as she grabbed a glass of champagne as well. "It looks like you've been preparing to feed Christmas dessert to an army."

Grams shrugged sheepishly. "I suppose I did get a bit carried away. When I realized how much I'd made, I decided to throw an impromptu party. We've been having a grand old time."

"I can see that," I said as I looked over the crowd of ladies in the kitchen. Most of them were paying no mind to me. Judging from the volume and frequency of their giggles, they'd all indulged in several glasses of champagne already.

For a moment, I considered coming back another time to ask Grams if she'd heard any updates about Simon's murder. I didn't want to put a damper on her party by asking about such a gruesome subject. But then, I figured I might as well ask now. Grams' friends didn't look like they were listening to my conversation with Grams anyway, and even if they were, they'd probably love the chance to spice up their conversations with the latest gossip.

Before I could even ask about the case, however, Grams brought it up.

"Any news on Simon?" she asked bluntly.

I sighed. "You know me too well, don't you?"

She winked at me. "Everyone in town knows you're looking into the case. There's no escaping it. You're Sunshine Springs' most popular amateur sleuth."

"Don't tell Mitch that," I groaned. "He caught me eavesdropping on his investigations last night at the station, and I'm pretty sure he's lobbying Santa to leave me nothing but a lump of coal this year."

"Luckily for you, I have more sway with Santa than Mitch does. Now spill the beans. What do you know?"

I was fairly certain that Grams already knew everything I could tell her, but I gave a quick rundown of the case to humor her. Grams told me what she knew as well, but unfortunately she didn't have any inside scoop to give me. All the talk at Sophia's Snips had apparently been about the supposed curse that the newspapers were proclaiming.

"It's the most ridiculous thing I've ever heard!" I said hotly when Grams mentioned the curse. "How can anyone truly believe that there's a Christmas curse, especially when there weren't actually any deaths in Sunshine Springs last Christmas! The whole thing is so obviously fabricated, but all the newspapers are latching onto it because the story is selling so well."

Grams shrugged mildly, apparently unperturbed by the fact that all of Northern California seemed to think that our town was cursed. "It'll pass," she said confidently. "These things always do."

"I don't have time to wait for this to pass!" I protested. "I need to make money over the holiday season, and I can't make money if no one visits my pie shop because they think the town is cursed. I'm not the only one worried about this, either. All of the business owners on Main Street will suffer if the tourists stay away."

Grams still looked unconcerned. "Once you solve the case, people will realize that it's not a curse and they'll come back to town. Don't you worry."

I let out an exasperated sigh. I loved Grams, but sometimes it drove me crazy how calm she was about everything. She never thought anything was an emergency, and, while I did have to admit that she was usually right about things working themselves out, this time she was wrong.

This *was* an emergency. Christmas itself was going to be ruined if this case wasn't solved soon, but there didn't seem to be any concrete clues as to who had actually strangled Simon Farrington. I took a long sip from my champagne flute and shook my head sadly at Grams.

"I don't know how I'm going to solve this case when there's no evidence."

Another one of the ladies in the kitchen set down her champagne flute with a definitive clink and shook her finger at me. "What do you mean, there's no evidence? Isn't it obvious? Vinny did it."

I looked over at the woman with mild interest. "He's a suspect, but there's no hard proof that he did anything."

The woman shook her hand in the air, causing her whole body to sway wildly back and forth. Alarmed, I stepped forward to steady her, worried that she was going to topple over from the effects of the champagne. She barely noticed me, though, and continued ranting.

"Vinny is not to be trusted," she said, her voice growing louder by the second. "He doesn't care about people at all. I don't doubt for a second that he would murder someone if they didn't fit his definition of being good for the environment. I'm all for taking care of the earth, but that guy has taken things too far. None of us are safe as long as he's walking the streets."

"You really think it was him?" I asked. "He's definitely suspicious, and I saw him arguing with Simon not long before the murder. But arguing in itself isn't proof that he's the guilty party."

I downed another sip of champagne, my frustration growing. Many times in the past, the gossip grapevine in Sunshine Springs had supplied me with clues that had helped me solve a case. But it seemed that this time, even the gossip grapevine didn't have any good information about what had happened. This woman wasn't telling me anything I didn't already know.

Still, she seemed determined to try to convince me and everyone else in the room of Vinny's guilt. She raised her voice even louder, and soon everyone in the kitchen, even Grams, was watching her as she pounded a fist on the counter for emphasis.

"You know what I saw the other day? I was walking down Main Street, minding my own business, when suddenly I heard yelling. I looked over and Vinny was yelling at a four year old child for using a plastic straw. Can you imagine? The poor kid had no idea what was going on. She'd just been minding her own business, drinking juice from her juice box, when this crazy man started screaming that she was killing the earth by using plastic. I don't care how much you care about the environment. No one should be yelling at a child like that!"

I winced, and nodded. I definitely agreed that a four-year-old child shouldn't be on the receiving end of an angry rant about straws. Knowing Vinny and how he acted, though, I couldn't say that I was surprised. He seemed to have no sense of when he needed to tone things down, and it was just like him to scream at a child. Still, as horrible as he'd acted toward that little girl, there was still no hard proof that he was the one who'd murdered Simon. All I had on Vinny was a few eyewitness accounts of his acting like a jerk. It was a pretty big jump to go from thinking that he was a jerk to thinking that he took someone's life.

I wasn't the only one who felt this way. Another of the women in Grams' kitchen waved her hand tipsily about and started giving her opinion on the matter. "Vinny has a good heart," she said, her voice filled with emotion in the way that only happens when someone has had too much champagne. "His methods are obnoxious and need refinement, I'll give you that. But I can't fault him for having a cause he believes in. If we all worked as hard as he does for a good cause, then our city, and our world, would be a better place."

"Our world would be a better place if people didn't murder each other," another woman piped in.

"Yeah, and if we didn't have to deal with the newspapers telling all the tourists that our town is cursed," said another person.

"Vinny didn't murder anyone. You can't pin that on him just because he has an opinion!" another voice said.

"He has more than just an opinion. He has an attitude problem!"

With that, the room erupted into a lively conversation. Soon, the noise was enough to draw in even the ladies who had been in the living room. Grams' kitchen was packed as everyone crowded in to debate whether Vinny was indeed responsible for Simon's murder. Sprinkles followed the crowd, and finally noticed I was there. He woofed happily and bounded over to greet me, not looking the least bit remorseful about the fact that he'd eaten far more sugar than he was normally allowed. I gave him a sharp look, but then rubbed him behind the ears.

"Come on, boy. I think it's time we made our exit. This party is getting a bit too lively for my tastes." I glanced over at Molly. "Are you coming with me?"

She shook her head. "No, I'll ride back with Rose. She lives right by the library, so she can easily drop me off at my car and save you the stop. Besides, I don't want to miss the rest of this conversation."

I shrugged, surprised that Molly was so interested in the twenty different opinions of Grams' twenty closest friends. "Suit yourself."

I gave Grams a quick hug and thanked her for the delicious treats, then took Sprinkles and started heading toward the front door. Before I could open it, however, someone else opened it from the outside. Surprised, I stepped back to see Theo pushing his way in, holding a case of wine in his arms. He looked just as surprised to see me as I was to see him.

"What are you doing here?" I asked, and he laughed.

"I could ask you the same thing. Do you always crash the parties your Grams has for her friends? I think you're about fifty years too young for this party."

I snorted at him. "I may be about fifty years younger than most of the guests, but they all have twice my spunk. You know Grams doesn't hang out with boring people."

"True enough. I didn't realize you'd be here, though. I might have been more willing to make a wine delivery if I'd known. But no matter. Your Grams still convinced me to bring out a case of my Pinot Noir by promising me some Christmas cookies. She called me about an hour ago, telling me that she needed an emergency supply of wine A.S.A.P."

Theo set down the case of wine and wiped at his brow dramatically, as though bringing in a case of wine from his winery had been so difficult that he might pass out from exhaustion at any moment. I rolled my eyes at him.

"I didn't realize I was going to be here, either. I came by to pick up Sprinkles and found this raging party going on, so I stayed for a bit to avail myself of those Christmas cookies you mentioned. I was just leaving, though. Things are getting a bit too spirited in there."

As if on cue, one of the ladies in the kitchen could be heard crying out at the top of her lungs, "We should storm the newspapers, and show them that they're the cursed ones if they slander our town!"

Theo's eyes widened, and then he laughed. "It does sound quite spirited. They're discussing the curse? That's all anyone in town's been talking about today."

I groaned. "With good reason. It's pretty awful. Don't tell me you're not worried about it! Surely it's going to affect your holiday sales."

Theo shifted uncomfortably from one foot to another, then shrugged. "I try not to worry about things I can't control."

For the first time in a long time, I found myself feeling genuinely annoyed with Theo.

"Right," I said saucily. "Of course you're not worried about it. Why would you be, when you're already so stinking wealthy? One season of bad sales won't make a big difference to you, so why would you care? For us mere mortals, however, a season of low sales is going to be devastating."

"I didn't mean it like that," Theo said weakly.

I crossed my arms. "No? Then how did you mean it?" Beside me, Sprinkles sighed and flopped down to the ground, as if settling in to endure a long, boring argument. I ignored him and kept my eyes trained on Theo.

Theo fished for the right words. "I know it won't be easy for a lot of people, but there's nothing I can do to change what the newspapers wrote. I do feel for people who are worried about their livelihood, but my being upset too isn't going to help things."

"It's not true that there's nothing you can do. You can help solve Simon's murder case."

Theo looked genuinely surprised by this statement. "How will that help?"

"If we can prove who actually murdered him and why they did it, I'm sure that people will see that this wasn't some curse randomly striking him dead."

Theo ran his fingers through his hair as he considered this. "I suppose you're right. But how can I help with that? You're the sleuth, Izzy. Not me."

I felt a strange sense of pride when I heard him call me a sleuth, just as I had when Molly complimented my sleuthing abilities. But I didn't have time to revel in compliments now. Not when our town's entire Christmas season was at stake. "You're a smart guy, Theo. Maybe if you think really hard about what you saw last night, something will stick out. Did Vinny say or do anything that indicated to you that he was about to kill Simon?"

Theo slowly shook his head. "Mitch has asked me the same question, and trust me: I've gone over and over everything in my mind. I feel somewhat responsible for Simon's death. Did I miss something I should have seen? Could I have prevented the murder? But no matter how hard I think about it, I just can't see how anything Vinny did gave any indication that he was going to kill Simon. Maybe it wasn't him. We don't know for sure."

"No, we don't," I agreed, my shoulders slumping in defeat. "But I can't see who else it might have been. I talked to Lynette, and she swore up and down that it wasn't her. She even denies that she vandalized Simon's decorations, even though Colleen claims to have video evidence of that."

Theo frowned. "Mitch told me this morning that Colleen does have the video evidence. She brought it in and he looked at it with his officers. They said that you can't see Lynette's face, but that her tattoo is plainly visible in one short portion of the footage."

I considered this. "Huh. I guess that doesn't surprise me that much since I don't see what reason Colleen would have to lie about it. But I am a bit surprised that Lynette would try to deny it was her even when she knew the tattoo was visible. Have you seen her tattoo? It's quite distinctive."

"I have seen it. She's quite dedicated to her love for her dog, I must say. Hey, maybe you should get a tattoo of Sprinkles on your wrist."

I rolled my eyes and punched Theo. "Okay, that's enough of all that. If you're just going to goof around, then I'm going to get going. I was on my way out, anyway, and I have things to do besides stand here and list all the reasons why I'm not going to get any tattoo, let alone one of my dog."

Theo only laughed harder at my indignation, and when I reached out to give him another annoyed punch, he caught my wrist to stop me before I could land the punch. But he didn't let go of my wrists right away. Instead, he took a step closer to me, until I could smell the distinctive scent of his aftershave. I blinked up at him, my heart suddenly pounding in my chest. His face was so close to mine...close enough that he could have dipped it down and kissed me. I was reminded of another moment several months ago, under the shade of an orange tree, where he had come close to kissing me.

Naturally, I panicked.

"What are you doing?" I asked, my eyes widening as I took a quick step backward.

Theo's eyes crinkled up into a smile. But it wasn't the goofy, silly smile he usually had when he was joking around about whatever was striking him as funny at the moment. Instead, it was a soulful smile that seemed to radiate true happiness.

"I'm just following the rules of Christmas," he said in an innocent tone of voice.

I frowned, and shook my head in confusion. "What in the world are you talking about?"

He let go of my wrists and pointed above my head. "You gotta watch where you're standing. Under the rules of Christmas, you're due for a kiss right about now."

I looked up, and saw to my horror that I was standing directly under a sprig of mistletoe that Grams had placed right in her entryway. I jumped back as if I'd just been told that I was standing in a fire, cursing under my breath the whole time. What had Grams been thinking, putting mistletoe there?

Theo was laughing now, and definitely in an amused way, not a soulful way. "I told you that you need to watch out for those!"

"No you didn't," I said hotly. I could feel my cheeks heating up with embarrassment as I realized that Theo had almost kissed me, and that I'd reacted rather like an immature schoolgirl when I'd realized that he was leaning in for a kiss. "Technically, all you told me was that I should put mistletoe in my pie shop."

Theo shrugged, unperturbed by my clarification. "You should. You'd have quite some entertainment when your customers stood under it without realizing it."

I huffed, and for good measure I took another step away from the mistletoe on Grams' ceiling. All thoughts of trying to discuss Simon's murder case with Theo had gone out the window. In fact, all thoughts of trying to discuss *anything* with Theo had gone out the window. I felt completely flustered, and I just wanted to escape to my car and go home. "I need to leave," I said in a firm voice. "Come on, Sprinkles."

I started marching toward the door, and I heard Sprinkles sigh as he fell into step behind me. Then I heard another sigh, this one from Theo.

"Izzy, don't leave mad. I was just playing around."

I paused and turned to face him, trying to keep a calm expression on my face and maintain my dignity. "It's fine," I said, hoping that my voice sounded steady and wasn't betraying the way my heart was pounding in my chest. "I'm not mad, but I do need to get going. It's been a long day, and I have a lot to do tomorrow."

Like solve a murder, and figure out how to keep my pie shop running in the middle of a supposed curse.

"I understand," Theo said softly. "But I didn't mean to upset you, honest. I was just having a bit of fun. And if there's anything I can do to help you with solving Simon's murder case, let me know. I'll do my best to help you and end this silly story about a curse."

I merely nodded, and then spun on my heel. I didn't trust myself to speak at that moment.

If I was honest, I wasn't exactly mad. I did feel quite emotional, but the emotion wasn't anger. It was more...longing.

I gulped and walked faster as I made my way to my car. I wasn't falling for Theo, was I? I'd promised myself I wouldn't do that. I had too much going on right now to be worrying about romance.

And yet, as I drove home, my thoughts bounced between how I was going to solve Simon's murder, and how I was going to get Theo Russo out of my head, where he seemed quite determined to stay.

CHAPTER TEN

The next day, I did my best to pour myself into my work at the Drunken Pie Café. If I was fully focused on baking and serving pies, then I wouldn't have time to think about Theo, right?

Unfortunately, the effects of the curse story seemed to have only spread, and business was even slower than the day before. I could only bake so many pies before I was just wasting ingredients baking pies I knew I would never sell. I could also only straighten the chairs and wipe down the display case so many times before I drove myself crazy from the repetition.

Tiffany, my part-time employee, had been scheduled to work all morning with me, and she did her best to cheer me up by making comments about how she was sure this was just the lull before the storm. But she and I both knew that something was wrong. Main Street shouldn't be this empty on a beautiful December afternoon. The weather was crisp but sunny, and it would have been the perfect day to get some Christmas shopping done.

But no one was shopping. All the tourists were hiding out from the curse, and unless something changed, and quickly, I knew that this was how my entire December was going to be. I had to get to work on Simon's murder case.

I was tempted to shut down the café completely, since business was so unbearably slow. But I couldn't keep myself from holding out hope that a group of tourists might come by who were blissfully unaware of the curse story. If nothing else, there would probably be a small but loyal contingent of Sunshine Springs locals stopping by later. And I knew Tiffany needed the hours. I couldn't keep the café open merely as a favor to her, of course, no matter how badly she needed the money. This was a business, not a charity, and if I wanted to stay in business I had to be careful how I managed things. But it was too early to throw in the towel on a good holiday season just yet, so I asked Tiffany if she could run the café for the afternoon and shut it down for me.

She was all too happy to do so, and I was all too happy to escape the four walls of the café. Normally, I loved that place. It was, after all, my baby. I'd dreamed of opening my own business for so long, and I'd built something special with a café that served boozy pies in the heart of wine country. But today I couldn't seem to stand inside the Drunken Pie Café without thinking of Theo's remarks about mistletoe.

I had to get out of there.

And if I wasn't going to be at the café, I knew I needed to spend my time working on Simon's case. I decided that the time had come to talk to Vinny, but I was nervous about doing so alone. He'd already proven that he could be quite, shall we say, *belligerent*. If he was indeed the murderer, then he'd probably be all too happy to strangle me too if I crossed him.

I decided that my first line of defense would be pie. Before I left the café, I chose a few slices of pie and placed them in a reusable box that I sometimes used to transport full pies. I didn't dare offer Vinny anything in a disposable container of any sort. If I attempted that, I was sure I wouldn't get a word in edgewise as he explained to me how I was destroying the earth. But surely, he couldn't refuse pie served in a completely eco-friendly manner.

I hoped not. But just in case my pie didn't impress him, I decided to use the buddy system and see if Molly could go with me. Once I settled into my car, I gave her a call, but her phone went straight to voicemail. I left her a quick message that I was going to be sleuthing that afternoon if she wanted to join, but I wasn't holding my breath that I'd hear back from her anytime soon. She was likely busy at the library, and if she wasn't busy there then she probably had her head stuck in wedding planning. Despite her proclamation the day before that she didn't need all of the crazy stuff the wedding magazines were pushing, I knew she wasn't going to completely give up on having a fairytale day—and I certainly didn't want to put a damper on her enthusiasm for planning that fairytale day. If she was busy, then I'd go sleuthing alone. It wouldn't have been my preference, given how nervous Vinny made me. But a sleuth did what a sleuth must to solve the case.

Besides, I wasn't completely alone. I had Sprinkles with me. I glanced over at the passenger seat of my car, where he sat and sleepily stared out the window. I reached over and ruffled his ears gently, chuckling as I watched him.

"Still recovering from that wild party last night, huh? I told you that you were gonna be feeling the effects of all that sugar today."

Sprinkles gave me a sheepish look, then settled deeper into the seat. I had a feeling that he wasn't regretting a thing, even though he'd been moving a little slowly today. He'd had quite a grand old time last night, and what was life without an over-the-top party now and then? He'd be feeling like his old self soon enough, and besides, I knew that he would move quickly if he really had to. If anyone threatened my life, as I worried that Vinny might, Sprinkles would quickly show that there was a ferocious side to his normally cuddly personality.

Feeling reassured, I started my car's engine and began to drive toward the outskirts of town, where the Sunshine Springs Christmas Tree Farm was located. I'd heard from more than one local that Vinny was spending a good deal of his time these days picketing in front of the farm, so I was hoping that I'd find him there.

I wasn't disappointed. When I got to the farm, Vinny was standing at the edge of the parking lot, holding up a cardboard sign painted with bright red letters that proclaimed "Death to Trees is Not the True Meaning of Christmas." He saw my car pulling in, and started marching over as he waved his sign wildly around.

I gulped. It looked like I was the only customer around at the moment, so I was about to bear the full brunt of Vinny's wrath. I didn't even see the owner, Stuart, walking around anywhere, although he couldn't have been too far. No doubt he was hiding out to avoid having to listen to Vinny's rants, and I couldn't blame him for that. Vinny had always made it clear that he hated the Christmas tree farm, but this year he was taking that hatred over the top, spending most of the day here and harassing every single person who walked onto the lot.

"Oh, it's you. The pie lady," Vinny said as I stepped out of my vehicle. He did not sound pleased to see who I was, and I figured he must at least suspect that I had ulterior motives for showing up at the tree farm. I was sure Mitch had already taken a statement from him, so Vinny was certainly well aware that he was a suspect in Simon's murder. And my reputation as an amateur sleuth preceded me, so I was sure he was also aware that I would be looking for clues that pointed to his involvement in the murder.

But the tension in the air wasn't anything a little pie couldn't overcome, right?

I gritted my teeth and said a silent prayer that this plan would work. Then I put a bright smile on my face and reached into the backseat of the car to carefully pull out the pie I had brought along. "Peppermint Schnapps chocolate cream pie?" I asked brightly. "Or perhaps a slice of cranberry vodka crumble?"

Vinny scowled at me, and Sprinkles, who had followed me out of the car, let out a low growl. I gave Sprinkles a look to silence him, at least for the moment. It made me feel better to know that my Dalmatian was there and feeling protective of me, but I didn't want him to scare Vinny off before I'd even had a chance to talk to the man.

"I'm not interested in your pie," Vinny snarled. "I don't eat takeout food. It's such a horrible industry for the environment! All those plastic forks and Styrofoam containers…ugh. Our poor Mother Earth."

I looked indignantly down at the container that I held in my hand. "I didn't use any plastic or Styrofoam containers to bring this pie out. It's in a reusable container, and I actually brought you a reusable plate and real silverware."

I'd been hoping to impress Vinny with my efforts, but he merely rolled his eyes at me. "So what? You did that for me because you know I actually care about the earth. But tell me, pie lady, do you use takeout containers in your café on a regular basis?"

"Well, yes," I stammered. "But how else would my customers be able to get orders to-go?"

Vinny crossed his arms. "They could slow down and eat their pie and drink their coffee in your café, instead of always needing to run off. You see? That's the problem with our society. Everything has to be quick, easy, and disposable. No one can imagine a world where the earth matters more than convenience. I refuse to eat any pie that came from a café that uses disposable containers. I don't care if that particular pie is in a reusable container."

I sighed, and put the pie back in my car. "I do care about the earth, Vinny. And I'm open to ideas on how to waste less in my business. But this all-or-nothing, in-your-face attitude you have isn't going to convert anyone to your cause. Trust me. That's not how battles are won."

"Maybe not in your war," Vinny snarled. "But I'm determined that things are going to drastically change in Sunshine Springs. Our town will lead the way to environmental salvation!"

Vinny fist-pumped the air, and Sprinkles looked up at me with a confused expression on his face. I shrugged slightly, unsure of what else to do. Vinny clearly wasn't interested in hearing my opinions about how to more effectively instigate change for the environment. I decided not to press him on that issue, and to instead ask him what he might know about Simon's untimely demise.

I crossed my arms and got a stern look on my face, deciding that sweet-talking wasn't the type of method that worked well with a man like Vinny. "I hear you and Simon were at odds about environmental responsibility as well."

Vinny rolled his eyes at me and threw his sign down on the ground in anger. "Here we go," he said in a venomous tone. "I knew the questions about Simon were coming. As soon as I saw that it was you getting out of the car, I knew you weren't here to buy a tree. You tracked me down so you can ask me a bunch of questions in hopes of proving that I killed Simon. Let me save you the time: I didn't kill him. But you know what? I hope people *do* think I'm the murderer."

I couldn't stop my jaw from dropping open in shock. "Why in the world would you want people to think you did it if you didn't?"

Vinny shrugged, and his eyes took on a defiant glint. "Because if people think I strangled Simon to save the environment, then maybe they'll be terrified enough of me that they'll change their own behavior to be more responsible. I would never actually kill anyone, because I don't want to spend the rest of my life in prison. But if people want to think that I'm a murderer, and thinking that helps our Mother Earth, then I'm not going to complain."

I found myself well and truly speechless. I wasn't sure that I'd ever been so fanatical about anything that I would have been okay with people thinking I had murdered someone over that issue. But Vinny stood in front of me looking completely unapologetic over the fact that he actually hoped people did think he was a murderer.

Undeterred by the astounded expression on my face, Vinny kept right on ranting. "I'll tell you one thing, though. I wish I had thought of the whole blackmail idea. I would have loved to have gotten a thousand dollars off of Simon over the fact that he cheated."

I narrowed my eyes at Vinny. "How did you know about the blackmail scheme?"

He sneered at me. "It's pretty much common knowledge at this point. Don't go thinking that the fact that I knew about it proves that I was involved in Simon's death. I guarantee you that if you go ask any local down on Main Street, they'll tell you all about the letter requesting the thousand dollars. That was a pretty smart request, if you ask me. Simon was so obsessed with that stupid decorating contest that he would have happily handed over the money to keep himself from being banned from the contest. If you're caught cheating, it's a lifetime ban."

"Seems like the committee in charge of the contest likes to issue lifetime bans."

Vinny shrugged. "Why not? If people can't behave enough to stay away from cheating or destroying other contestants' property, they don't deserve a second chance. Of course, I wouldn't have asked for money if I'd blackmailed Simon. I would have forced him to choose more eco-friendly decorations and make a donation to an environmental activist group in exchange for my silence. I could have done it, too. I knew he'd cheated. It just never occurred to me to use that knowledge to force him into helping the environment."

I was silent for a few more moments, trying to process all of this information. Was Vinny's devil-may-care attitude a cover up? Or was he sincerely bummed that he hadn't thought of blackmailing Simon before someone else? I gave Vinny a long, hard stare, but he didn't seem bothered by this. In fact, he hadn't seemed all that bothered by anything I'd said or done since I'd arrived at the tree farm. The only thing that had gotten a rise out of him was my attempt to serve him pie.

Something was strange about all of this, but was it related to the murder? Or was Vinny just a strange person?

"Cat got your tongue?" he finally said in a sing-song voice, obviously making fun of the fact that he'd rendered me speechless.

I cleared my throat and stood tall, determined not to let him get the best of me. "How did you know that Simon cheated?"

He shrugged. "It was obvious, if you looked at his decorations. The committee puts out a theme for the decorating contest every year, and this year's theme is Gingerbread and Gumdrops. People usually don't start decorating until the theme comes out, because they want to plan their whole decorating scheme around that theme. If they do actually start decorating before the theme comes out, it's just basic stuff, like outlining their houses with lights. The committee reveals the theme to everyone at the same time so that everyone has a fair chance to plan and execute their master decorating plan."

I cocked an eyebrow at Vinny. "You sure know a lot about this decorating contest, for someone who's so opposed to Christmas."

"I'm not opposed to Christmas. I'm opposed to Christmas decorations. And that's precisely why I know so much about the contest. I've been trying for years to have the contest banned in Sunshine Springs."

I shook my head slightly. "You must be really popular at parties."

"I don't go to many parties."

I resisted the urge to rudely roll my eyes. "Why am I not surprised?"

Vinny ignored me and continued his explanation of Simon's cheating scandal. "Anyway, the theme was only announced three days ago, but within hours Simon's whole yard had been transformed into a gumdrop and gingerbread wonderland. Anyone who took one look at his yard would have instantly known that he knew about the theme ahead of time. Luckily for him, I don't think many people looked at his yard. Everyone was too busy making their own plans. Everyone except Lynette Moir. She was obsessed with seeing what Simon was doing, and she would have known that he cheated just by looking at his yard the day after the theme was announced. If you want to know who murdered him, I suggest talking to her."

"I have talked to her. She swears she didn't do it, just like you do." I sighed, then fixed a stern glare on Vinny. "Someone isn't telling the truth here. I just have to figure out who it is."

But he once again seemed completely unbothered by my attempts to intimidate him. "I'm telling the truth, pie lady. I have nothing to hide. In fact, go ask Colleen. She'll tell you all about Lynette. Simon and Colleen both couldn't stand her, and I'm sure that Colleen knows deep down that it was Lynette who strangled Simon. To be honest, I don't know why she strangled him instead of just taking the blackmail money and enjoying it. My guess is that her hatred for Simon overcame her in that moment, and she couldn't keep herself from giving in to that hatred."

I gave Vinny a doubtful look. "It would take a lot of hatred to make someone actually kill someone."

Vinny shrugged nonchalantly. "Lynette had a lot of hatred stored up in that black heart of hers."

Sprinkles growled, and I had to agree with him that Vinny was acting suspicious. Lynette had definitely struck me as the obnoxious type, but I thought Vinny was stretching a bit by saying that she had a black heart. His heart seemed much blacker than hers, if you asked me. After all, he was standing in front of me casually saying that he didn't care if people thought he had murdered Simon. That sounded pretty black to me.

But arguing with Vinny about who had the blacker heart wasn't going to get me any new information on Simon's murder case. I swallowed back the abundance of snide remarks I wanted to make, and tried to think instead of what other information I might be able to get from him. He did know a lot about the decorating contest and all of the parties involved. Was it possible that Vinny knew of someone else who had been aware of Simon's cheating ways? If there was anyone else who had known, I needed to know about it. I truly believed that I could figure out who was responsible for the murder if I could figure out who was responsible for that note. Most likely, the note writer was the murderer. But even if they weren't, and someone else had happened to strangle Simon when he was going to meet the note-writer, then the note-writer would have at least seen something.

Someone knew something, I was sure of that. And I had to find out what that something was.

"Did anyone other than you and Lynette know that Simon had cheated on the contest?" I asked, trying to keep my voice from sounding too annoyed. If I wanted to get information out of Vinny, then I needed to at least attempt to be nice to him.

But my attempts to act civil didn't seem to impress Vinny. He bent over to pick up his sign that he'd thrown on the ground, and his voice sounded bored as he spoke. He was clearly done with this conversation. "I dunno. Colleen must have known, but it wouldn't have made any sense for her to threaten Simon like that. I'm not sure if they had a joint bank account, but I am sure that if she wanted a thousand dollars of his money to spend, there were easier ways for her to get it than sending him a blackmail note to meet her on Main Street."

"So you and Lynette were essentially the only ones who knew about the cheating?"

Vinny brushed some dirt off of his sign, then looked up at me with narrowed eyes. "What are you implying, pie lady?"

I crossed my arms, refusing to cower in the face of his obvious anger. He hadn't cowered at all when I tried to be firm with him, so I definitely wasn't going to cower for him. There was no way I was letting him get the upper hand in this discussion.

"I'm not implying anything," I said in a breezy tone. "I'm just asking if anyone else knew about the cheating."

"Not that I know of," Vinny said, his eyes betraying the first hint of worry I'd seen. "But that doesn't mean there wasn't anyone else. Lynette's just the only one I know of. There very well might be more." Then he stuck his chin out defiantly. "But like I said, Lynette's probably the one who killed Simon. She has a black heart."

He held his sign up with one hand, and traced a heart shape in the air with the other while mouthing the words "black heart."

I bit back a sigh of frustration. I didn't want Vinny to know that the lack of information in this case was getting to me, but it was. I was beginning to think that I'd learned all I could from Vinny, and that worried me. Where did I go from here? Lynette and Vinny had both been far less than helpful in sorting all of this out. Who else might be able to give me some clues?

Mitch might know something, but I doubted he would be willing to share what he knew with me. Colleen was another person I needed to talk to, but I didn't feel right about pestering her so soon after she'd lost her husband in such a tragic manner. I was sure that having to give the police a statement was traumatic enough. She probably wouldn't appreciate having an amateur sleuth knocking down her door as well.

But I couldn't give up. Not when Sunshine Springs was on the verge of having its entire Christmas shopping season ruined. I was depending on Christmas sales, and so were my fellow business owners. I wasn't going to let them down.

I frowned, wishing that Molly was there with me. Now, more than ever, I felt that I could use my best friend to bounce ideas off of. I'd had a lot of success as an amateur sleuth since moving to Sunshine Springs, but I was worried that this was the case that was finally going to stump me. Talking things through with Molly often helped me sort out what I needed to do next, but Molly was so busy these days. I didn't want to dampen her enthusiasm for her wedding planning by dumping all my detective problems on her, but then who could I talk to?

My inner worries were interrupted by Vinny sticking his sign right in my face. "Enough with the interrogation, pie lady. I have work to do. These trees deserve justice!"

I took a step back, wrinkling my nose at him and his sign, which was now quite dirty after spending a few minutes on the dusty ground. "I'm not sure what work you have to do. There aren't any customers here now anyway."

Vinny glanced around, seeming surprised to realize that I was right. The parking lot was completely empty except for my car, Vinny's car, and Stuart's car. For a moment, Vinny actually smiled.

"I suppose there aren't. This is good news. Perhaps my valiant efforts are finally paying off, and people are realizing that killing trees isn't the meaning of Christmas!"

Neither is killing people, I thought, still feeling appalled at Vinny's hope that people would think he'd killed Simon and would be frightened into taking better care of the environment.

But I held my tongue. Vinny wasn't the type of person you could have a civil conversation with when it came to his environmental crusade. Instead of dignifying him with a response, I turned to start getting back into my car. He wasn't interested in my pie, and I wasn't interested in talking to him any longer. I needed to go somewhere quiet to think and figure out what my next move was going to be.

But just as I was climbing into my car, Stuart, the owner of the Christmas tree farm, came rushing over.

"Hey!" Stuart shouted. "Get away from her, Vinny! I've told you to stay off my property and stop bothering my customers!"

Vinny looked up and sneered at Stuart. "It's a free country."

"Yes, a free country that allows for private property ownership. Now get off my land before I call the cops."

"Mitch can't spare an officer to come down here and push me around," Vinny retorted. "Not when there's a murderer on the loose."

Stuart roared in anger and pulled his cell phone out of his pocket. "Should we find out?"

Vinny rolled his eyes. "Another day, perhaps. Right now, I was leaving anyway. I'm starving and I need to go get something to eat."

I refrained from making a sarcastic comment about how there was plenty of pie available to eat. I didn't want to waste any more time on Vinny. He clearly had nothing else important to tell me.

Vinny had sauntered off, with Sprinkles letting out a series of low growls in his wake. I couldn't blame my dog. Something about Vinny was definitely off. Whether it was the fact that he was a murderer or just the fact that he was an obnoxious human being, well, that was a whole other question.

Stuart gave me an apologetic look. "I'm so sorry about that. I've been trying to keep him off my land, but every time I turn around he's snuck back on and is bothering another customer. It's like playing whack-a-mole. I hope he didn't bother you too much."

I shook my head, suddenly feeling very sorry for Stuart. I couldn't imagine having to deal with Vinny every day. "He didn't bother me. Well, not too much. I actually came out here looking for him. I wanted to talk to him about Simon's murder, but he didn't have that much to tell me. That's not that surprising, I guess. If he's innocent he probably doesn't know anything, and if he's guilty he's certainly not going to be shouting that from the rooftops."

Stuart snorted and let out a bitter-sounding laugh. "Well, I'd be shocked if he was guilty. I have no idea how he would find time to commit a murder when he's always here, scaring off customers. Everything he's saying isn't true, anyway! My trees aren't killing the environment, and besides that, I donate a portion of my profits every year to a charity that funds the planting of new trees all over the world."

"I didn't know you did that. That's really cool."

Stuart nodded proudly. "Of course I do. Taking care of Mother Earth is important to me. Many people don't know that real Christmas trees are actually good for the environment. These trees aren't just cut down from wild forests! They're grown on Christmas tree farms, and they're grown in places were no other crops would be able to grow. While they're growing, they're absorbing carbon dioxide and producing oxygen. Then, when a tree is big enough to cut down, a new one is immediately planted in its place. It's a beautiful way to celebrate the holidays while also benefitting the earth."

I raised a surprised eyebrow. "I had no idea you were so passionate about this."

Stuart nodded his head enthusiastically. "I'm very passionate about it. This tree farm isn't just a job to me. It's my life's work. I don't know if you know this, but my father owned this farm before me. I took over the mantle from him when he passed away, and I'm proud to have been in charge of supplying trees to Sunshine Springs and the surrounding communities for over ten years now. Of course, if things keep going the way they have been, I might not be able to continue running this business."

I felt a pang of sympathy for him. The anguish on his face made the wrinkles around his eyes and mouth even deeper, and he looked quite tired.

"Has Vinny really been keeping that many customers away?" I asked. "I thought most people in town just rolled their eyes at his overzealous protests."

Stuart shrugged. "Well, he hasn't helped things. People like to come have a fun family experience when they pick out a Christmas tree. They want to drink some hot chocolate and take some photos in front of the big wooden Santa Claus I have out front. They don't want some guy waving cardboard signs in their face and telling them that they're destroying the earth." Stuart let out a long sigh. "But Vinny isn't the only problem I've got this year."

I raised a questioning eyebrow. "What other problems do you have?"

"You should know," Stuart said. "Don't tell me you haven't been affected by the Christmas curse."

I groaned. "I don't know any business owner in Sunshine Springs who hasn't been affected."

"Exactly," Stuart said in a mournful tone. "No one is making sales, and even though it's only been a couple days, people are panicking. Everyone is hanging on to every dollar they have, which means that they aren't buying Christmas trees. It's a downward spiral, and it's going to affect every single person who lives in Sunshine Springs."

Stuart's voice was rising with every word he said, and the panic emanating off of him hung so thickly in the air that I almost felt I could have reached out and cut it with the pie knife that still sat on my backseat. I felt bubbles of anger rising within me. Whoever had murdered Simon hadn't just needlessly cut his life short. They had also brought down the entire town.

But I wasn't going to let this continue.

"No!" I said firmly.

Stuart looked up in surprise. "No?" he said, trying hard not to sniffle, although it was clear to me that the poor old man was on the verge of tears.

"No," I repeated. "Sunshine Springs is stronger than any murder or curse or anything else the world can throw at us. I moved to this town because I wanted to be part of a community, and that's what I've found here: a community. If we all stick together, we can make it through this."

Stuart gave me a weary look. "Those are nice words, Izzy. But they're only words. At the end of the day, we all still need money to pay our rent or mortgage and put food on the table."

"It's more than just words," I said, standing taller. Beside me, Sprinkles barked enthusiastically, and I smiled down at him, grateful for his show of support. "I'm not just saying we're going to make it through this. I'm going to personally help us make it through this!"

Stuart still looked skeptical. "But how?"

"By finding Simon's murderer," I declared. "Once the murderer is caught, and there's a reasonable explanation for all of this, then all the newspapers will be forced to admit that there's no substance to this Christmas curse story. The tourists will see how silly it all is, and they'll return to Sunshine Springs, eager to taste our delicious food and wine and buy the unique gifts we offer in our shops. And once all the Sunshine Springs locals are making money again, they'll be happy to come buy Christmas trees from you."

Stuart looked slightly less skeptical. "You really think so? But how long will it take to solve the murder case? The holiday season is short, and we've already lost a few days of sales. We can't lose many more without it being too late to salvage things."

"I know I have to work quickly," I said. "But I can do this. I *know* I can."

Beside me, Sprinkles once again barked, giving me a vote of confidence. I looked down at him with a smile, hoping that my smile would hide the actual nervousness that I felt deep inside. This wasn't going to be easy, and I still wasn't sure what my next step would be.

But Stuart needed me. Sunshine Springs needed me. I wasn't going to let them down.

I hadn't failed before, and I wasn't going to fail now. I would find a way to solve this case and set things right in Sunshine Springs once again.

"Don't worry," I reassured Stuart. "In a few days this will all be over. In fact, I'm so confident that it will be that I'm going to buy a Christmas tree for my café right now. I'm not afraid to spend the money, because I know the holiday sales are coming."

In reality, I was terrified to spend the money. But I figured that there was no better way to force myself to make good on my word to solve the case then to put my money where my mouth was.

Stuart's face lit up. "Really? You're going to buy a tree."

"Sure am." Then I glanced at the pie I'd brought with me. "You wouldn't happen to like peppermint schnapps, would you? I've got a whole peppermint schnapps chocolate cream pie here that Vinny refused to eat."

Stuart's eyes widened. "Vinny wouldn't eat it? That guy is crazier than I thought. Who would turn down a peppermint schnapps chocolate cream pie? I'd love a slice."

"That's the spirit!" I said. "Let's fuel up on pie, and then you can help me pick out the perfect tree for my café."

Stuart practically beamed as we walked back toward his office to share some pie. As the first pepperminty bite hit my tongue, I couldn't help but sigh happily.

For the first time since Simon's murder, I felt a little prickle of hope that the Christmas spirit was indeed still alive and well in Sunshine Springs. It just needed a tiny bit of encouragement to make its appearance.

I, for one, was going to encourage it as much as possible.

CHAPTER ELEVEN

I'd never met anyone as knowledgeable about Christmas trees as Stuart. As we searched for the perfect tree for my café, he spouted off facts about how the Christmas tree tradition had originated, as well as plenty of opinions on which varieties of evergreens made the best decorative trees. Normally, I couldn't stand people who acted like walking trivia books, but there was nothing the least bit annoying about the way Stuart spoke of Christmas trees. His voice rose and fell with enthusiasm, and his face radiated joy. I could tell that he truly loved his Christmas tree business, and that, contrary to what Vinny seemed to think, Stuart did care about the sustainability of live Christmas trees.

I originally planned to choose a small, modest tree that could be placed unobtrusively in the corner of my café. But Stuart's enthusiasm for the trees wore off on me, and I found myself choosing a bushy, six foot giant that would dominate the café. I worried as Stuart strapped it onto my car that I had made a mistake, but I wasn't going to switch it out for a different tree at that point.

The thing dwarfed the roof of my small sports coupe, and I was a bit worried about how I would manage to get it off the car and into my café. Sprinkles eyed the tree, and me, suspiciously. He continued to eye me suspiciously when I stopped by a local store to pick up some ornaments and lights for the tree, leaving him waiting just outside the front door. I tried to call Theo to see if he'd come meet me at the café to help unload it. But the call went to voicemail, so I tried Molly. She might not be as strong as Theo, but between the two of us I was sure we could manage. And if she couldn't do it, then maybe she could send Scott.

But apparently no one was answering their phones today. Feeling a bit lonesome, and wondering how in the world I was going to get the tree off the car, I headed down to my café. I sped up a little as I drove, hoping I might still catch Tiffany. She had texted me a little while before to say that she thought it might be best if we close early. The afternoon rush of locals had finished, and our late afternoon and early evening business was almost all tourists. According to Tiffany, not a single tourist had set foot inside the café today, so it didn't make sense to stay open.

I knew that closing early meant less money for Tiffany, and I appreciated the fact that she was looking out for the café, even though she herself would lose out on a few hours of wages. She was a conscientious employee like that, and I was lucky to have her. It had taken a while to find someone I could trust, but it was nice to not have to run the café completely by myself anymore. Plus, if she was still there when I arrived, she could help me with this tree.

As I drove up in front of the café, however, my hopes were dashed. A cheerful, hand-painted sign proclaimed "CLOSED" in colorful letters. The letter "O" was painted to look like a pie, giving the sign an adorable, whimsical touch. I'd commissioned a local artist to make the sign for me, and I did love how it had turned out. But right now, I was bummed to be looking at it. Not only was it a reminder that there wasn't enough business to keep the shop open, but that sign, along with the fact that the lights were all off inside the café, meant that I had almost certainly missed Tiffany. Was I really going to have to get this Christmas tree inside by myself?

For a moment, I considered just leaving the tree on top of my car and driving home. Surely, by the next day I'd get a hold of someone who could help me take it down. But the thought of driving around with a Christmas tree on top of my small car any more than I already had was not appealing. Not to mention the fact that I wanted to get the tree up and decorated so that the task was done. I planned to hit the ground running tomorrow, spending every spare second of my time chasing down Simon's murderer. Best to get this tree decorated now, even if that did mean I had to get it inside alone. I was sure to look ridiculous doing so, but that was the one bright side to the fact that Main Street was completely deserted: there would be no witnesses to my attempt to drag a giant tree into my café.

I inched my car forward so that it was parked as close as humanly possible to the front door. Then I unlocked the door and propped it wide open using one of the café tables. I made sure there was a clear path to the corner where I wanted to set up the tree, and then I carried in the tree stand and boxes of ornaments that I'd purchased. I tried to think of anything else that might need to be done before I brought the tree in, but finally I could procrastinate no longer. After taking one more glance at my phone to make sure no one had called me back to say they were on their way to help me with the tree, I resigned myself to my fate.

I would move the tree alone.

I carefully cut the twine that had secured the tree to my car, thankful that at least Stuart had wrapped the branches tightly in netting. It made maneuvering the mammoth conifer easier, but the thing was still quite unwieldy. Getting it off the car without having it completely crash to the ground would be tricky. After much internal debate over the best angles and method for unloading a tree from one's car by oneself, I decided to just go for it. Sprinkles whined at me, and I think if he had been human he would have been covering his face with his hands. He clearly didn't think this was a good idea, but I didn't see any other options.

I figured it was best to get the trunk on the ground first, so I reached up to yank the trunk sideways and down. The thing moved much faster than I'd been expecting, and I gave a little shriek as the tree slid downward. I winced as I grabbed for it, hoping that I wasn't going to have tiny pine needle scratches all over my car. Somehow, I managed to keep the tree upright after it landed with a thud on its stump of a trunk. I nearly fell over myself in the process, but when everything finally came to a standstill, both the tree and I were still standing. Sprinkles whined again, although he sounded slightly less concerned. At least the tree was off the car at this point.

"And now, to get this thing inside," I muttered.

There was no graceful way to handle the task ahead. I huffed and puffed, and dragged that green behemoth toward the café's front door. I almost fell over several times, and despite attempting to keep the tree relatively upright, I found myself practically buried underneath it as I inched forward. My scalp prickled, no doubt full of pine needles, and I was sure that there was going to be a nice, long trail of pine needles from my car to my café.

No matter. They were easy enough to sweep up. I didn't care about the mess in that moment. All I cared about was getting the tree inside before anyone saw me. I could feel sweat beading up on my forehead, but my hands were too full of tree to be able to wipe it away. I was afraid that if I let go of my grip for even a moment, that I'd never get the tree lifted off the ground again. My only consolation was that Main Street was still deserted, and no one was witnessing this debacle.

"Need a hand with that?"

I shrieked, and in my surprise I dropped the tree. With the mass of pine branches no longer obscuring my view, I could see Mitch standing right in front of me, his expression a mixture of concern and amusement.

So much for no one witnessing the Izzy versus pine tree struggle. I was pretty sure that the pine tree had just won, and I must have looked like quite a sight. I noticed that I'd somehow torn the sleeve of my shirt, and not only that but it was also covered in some sort of sticky pine sap. My hair had almost completely unraveled from the bun it had been in, and when I wiped at my face, my arm came away full of sweat, dirt, and pine needles.

"Um, a hand would be nice," I said sheepishly.

Mitch shot me one more amused glance before easily hoisting the tree over his shoulder and carrying it through the open front door of the Drunken Pie Café. "Where do you want it?"

I pointed to the corner where the tree stand stood waiting, and Mitch easily pivoted to carry the tree over and drop it in the tree stand. I went over to secure the tree into the stand while Mitch held it steady, all the while still cursing under my breath that my tree-moving fiasco had been witnessed by one of my good friends.

It wasn't until the tree was fully secured that I finally stood up and faced Mitch again. I tried not to look uncomfortable, but it was hard to project confidence when I was still covered in the remnants of the pine tree that now proudly stood in the corner of my café.

"Why didn't you call someone to help you?" Mitch asked. "I swear, your penchant for doing everything yourself gets you into all kinds of trouble."

"There's nothing wrong with being an independent woman," I said defensively. "But as a matter of fact, I did call someone. I called both Molly and Theo, but no one was answering their phones."

"You could have called me." Mitch sounded a little hurt, and I had to resist the urge to roll my eyes. For all their macho bravado, men sure could have some fragile egos sometimes.

"I didn't want to bother you when I know you're so busy working on Simon's murder case."

This wasn't exactly the truth. I didn't want to bother Mitch because I knew the murder case was at the forefront of his mind right now, which meant he'd be hyperaware of anything I said or did that clued him in to the fact that I was trying to solve the case as well. He must have understood that this was my real motivation for avoiding him, because he gave me an exasperated look as he sank into one of my café chairs.

"I'm not an idiot, Izzy. I know that you're running around asking Lynette and Vinny questions."

I sank into a café chair as well. "Ugh. I can't keep anything a secret in this town. Who told you?"

"Lynette told me that you'd come by, because she wanted me to know that she had been wrongly accused and didn't appreciate that she was being harassed because of it."

"I didn't harass her! She invited me in for tea!"

Mitch shrugged. "She is a dramatic one. I'll give you that. As for Vinny—he didn't have to tell me anything. I knew that if you were talking to Lynette, you'd be talking to him as well."

I made a face. "So that's why you came here, then? To tell me to stay out of the case?"

To my surprise, Mitch shook his head. "No, actually. You *should* stay out of the case, but I didn't come here to tell you that. I came here about something else."

Even though I was the one who had been caught doing unauthorized sleuthing, Mitch suddenly looked like the uncomfortable one. He shifted his gaze to the ceiling, refusing to make eye contact with me. He also loudly cracked his knuckles several times, a surefire sign that he was feeling agitated.

"Something else?" I prompted.

He sighed. "Yes, well…the thing is…"

He looked at me briefly, then looked up at the ceiling again. I didn't think I'd ever seen him looking this nervous.

"Mitch, whatever it is, just spit it out. I'm your friend. What could you possibly have to say to me that's so concerning?"

For a brief moment, I felt fear grip my heart. Had something happened to Grams? But no, that didn't make sense. If he had bad news to tell me about my grandmother, he would have told me right away. He was a professional, and would have known better than to delay the inevitable by spending time on setting up a Christmas tree. But if it wasn't bad news about someone I loved, why was he acting so hesitant?

"Mitch?" I tried again.

He sighed, cracked his knuckles, and finally looked at me. "The thing is…you and Alice are good friends, right?"

I frowned, confused. "Yes, of course. Not as close as Molly and I, but I see her quite often and I'd say she's one of my better friends in Sunshine Springs."

Mitch's face turned red, but he pressed forward. "So, you talk with her regularly?"

I narrowed my eyes at him, suddenly realizing what this was all about. "Fairly regularly. Why?"

Mitch shifted uncomfortably in his seat. "I was just wondering if she's said anything about me."

I grinned at him. "Why would she be talking about you?"

I knew the answer, and Mitch knew I knew it. He gave me a frustrated glare, but I persisted in staring innocently back at him. I couldn't let this opportunity pass me by. Sheriff Mitchell McCoy, arguably the toughest man in town, was flustered by sweet, quiet Alice Warner. Everyone knew by now that the two of them were dancing around the fact that they liked each other, but I wanted Mitch to quit dancing. I wanted him to outright admit it.

He cracked his knuckles several times but didn't speak. He was probably hoping that I would break down and say something first, but I wasn't going to cave. I had him in the hot seat and he knew it. If he wanted my help wooing Alice, and he obviously did, then he was going to have to say so.

"Oh fine," he finally said. "It's not like it's some big secret. Alice and I have been spending quite a bit of time together lately, and it seems that something, er, romantic is developing between us."

"Go on," I said encouragingly, my smile widening.

"Well, I like where things are going. To be honest, Alice was never on my radar as a potential girlfriend. She's always been a decent enough friend, but I didn't look that closely at her. She was just sort of the nice gal who ran a café that serves really good muffins and lunch sandwiches. But then the last murder case I worked on forced me to spend time getting to know her better. She's really quite an incredible person."

Mitch paused, his cheeks turning downright crimson. I felt a twinge of sympathy. The poor guy was head over heels, and didn't know what to do with himself. I stood, and held up one finger.

"Wait just a moment. Hold that thought, and I'll get us some pie to munch on while we talk. Lord knows I have enough of it left over since there aren't any tourists around these days."

I went to grab a full spiked Christmas pie as well as a bottle of wine. Then, when Sprinkles whined in a not-so-subtle manner, I grabbed some non-boozy strawberry pie for him. I set both pies down on the café table between Mitch and me, and served Mitch a generous slice of the spiked pie before giving Sprinkles an equally generous slice of the strawberry pie. My pup had been a good buddy to me today, and I felt like he deserved a treat. Then, I poured Mitch and myself generous glasses of wine. A few moments later, we were both munching pie and sipping wine in silence. Mitch gradually looked a little less red, and after a few more bites of pie he finally seemed ready to speak again.

"I guess I was hoping that you could tell me if she's said that she likes me? I want to officially ask her out on a date, but I'm worried that I'm misreading all her signals. What if she doesn't actually like me, and she laughs in my face?"

I took a bite of pie and gave Mitch a kind smile. "First of all, Alice isn't the type of person to laugh in anyone's face. She's much too nice for that."

I saw the tension in Mitch's shoulders relax a little. "True."

"Second of all, I haven't talked to her much lately, because I've been busy both with helping Molly wedding plan and with trying to figure out who murdered Simon."

Mitch frowned, but I merely shrugged at him.

"I don't see the point in denying that I'm sleuthing. You already know, and I don't think anyone can blame me for being extra-concerned about this case. Not when this supposed Christmas curse is ruining holiday sales for everyone."

Mitch opened his mouth like he was going to say something else, but I held up a hand to stop him.

"Wait a minute. We can argue later about the murder case and whether I should be doing detective work. Right now, we're talking about you and Alice."

"But you said you haven't talked to her all that much lately."

"I haven't. But it doesn't matter whether I've talked to her or whether she's said anything to anyone about her feelings for you. The important thing here is that you know in your heart that you care about her. If you have feelings for her, then you need to man up and tell her. Women like that, you know? We like it when a guy takes a chance on us."

Mitch actually laughed. "Is that so? Because I took a chance on telling you that I liked you, and you completely rebuffed me."

I laughed as well. "Fair enough. But you and I are all wrong for each other. We make great friends, but we'd drive each other crazy in a relationship."

Mitch laughed a little harder. "We drive each other crazy just in a friendship. A relationship would have been a complete disaster. I can see that now. We're both too hardheaded for it to work between us."

I actually felt lighter when he said those words. I had worried for a while that he would hold a bit of a grudge against me for not dating him. But he seemed to have realized that it was for the best, and it seemed we would remain friends.

Well, we would remain friends as long as he didn't tear my head off for interfering with his murder cases. But even though he complained nonstop about my detective work, my head currently remained intact. I had a sneaking suspicion that he didn't hate my interference in his cases as much as he claimed he did. I did have a talent for sleuthing, after all, and that talent had helped him solve a number of cases.

But right now, we weren't talking about murder cases. We were talking about Alice. Even though Alice hadn't actually said anything to me about Mitch, I had seen the way she looked at him lately. I would have bet money on the fact that she liked him. And he obviously liked her. The two of them just needed to stop denying their feelings.

"I'm telling you," I said, shaking a forkful of pie in Mitch's direction. "You just need to get over your fear and talk to her. The next time you see her, tell her you'd like to pursue things further with her, and then ask her out on an official date. I think you'll be surprised at how eagerly she responds."

Mitch ate a few more bites of pie in silence as he considered my words. Finally, he looked up at me and nodded. "You're right. I need to just take the chance and ask her. I think she does like me, and even if she doesn't, she's worth fighting for. She's worth taking a chance for."

"That's the spirit," I said with a grin. I reached over to refill his wine glass, which he'd drained quite quickly amidst his nerves about Alice.

After a few more sips of wine and bites of pie, he was looking quite relaxed. I wondered if I might be able to convince him to tell me whether there were any updates on the case. After all, I'd helped him with his Alice question. Surely, that had earned me the right to ask a question of my own. I took a deep breath and decided to just go for it.

"So, since you're here, any updates on Simon's murder case?"

Mitch gave me a frown so big that it was almost comical. "Don't think you can butter me up to talk about the case just because you helped me work through what I should do about Alice. You know I don't discuss ongoing cases."

"Hmph. You don't discuss them with me. But I know you always tell Theo what's going on."

Mitch rolled his eyes heavenward. "Okay, so I talk to him more than I talk to you. But he's been my best friend for a long time. And besides, when I tell him what's going on with a case, he doesn't immediately run off and try to interview all the suspects."

To my utter dismay, I felt tears prickling at the back of my eyelids. I blinked quickly, trying to force them away. I didn't want to get all emotional in front of Mitch, but the feeling of despair rising within me had taken me completely by surprise.

"Can you blame me for being concerned about this?" I asked hotly, trying to sound like I was angry instead of on the verge of tears. "Until Simon's murder is solved, no one in Sunshine Springs is making any holiday sales. I've vowed to solve this case and save the Christmas season, and I don't care how much you complain. I'm not going to stay out of things. This town matters to me. Our Christmas season matters to me. I'm a good detective, and I know I can help with this. I'm not just going to stand by and do nothing."

Mitch gave me a long, hard look over the rim of his wine glass, and I could tell he was considering what to say next. I prepared myself to defend against what I was sure would be a long rant about how I was putting myself in danger, but to my surprise that wasn't what he said when he did finally speak.

"Tell you what. I'll make you a deal."

"A deal?" I squeaked out, confused.

He nodded. "I don't like you working on these cases, but I know that no matter how much I beg you to stay out of things, you're not going to listen, anyway. I might as well accept that and make use of your help, because you're right. This case does need to be solved quickly, or Christmas in Sunshine Springs is going to be ruined."

My jaw dropped. "Are you telling me you're not going to forbid me from working on this case?"

Mitch chuckled. "I'm not going to forbid you from working on the case. What's the point? I can do all the forbidding in the world, and you won't listen. I might as well let you in on what few clues I do have and see if you can make sense of them."

I could hardly believe what I was hearing. "You're actually going to give me information on the case?"

"Yes, but it's going to cost you."

I narrowed my eyes at him. "Cost me what?"

"I'll let you in on the case and share clues with you, if you help me plan a date for Alice. You know her pretty well, and you must know what women like in a date, right? Help me figure out where to take her and how to really impress her, and I'll let you help on the case."

I couldn't help but laugh. "Wow, you really are smitten, aren't you?"

Mitch looked slightly embarrassed, but not as much as before. This time, his cheeks didn't turn red and he didn't avoid eye contact with me. "Can you blame me? She's a pretty great person."

"She is," I agreed. "Tell you what: do you have anything going on this afternoon?"

"Not at the moment. I'm off work for the day, and Alice had an appointment down at Sophia's Snips. She warned me she'd probably be there for several hours." Mitch rolled his eyes at me. "I swear. I don't know what it is you women all do in that salon for hours on end. Does it really take that long to get a haircut?"

I shook a finger at him. "Okay, first lesson: none of that sort of talk. The answer is yes, it does take that long to get a haircut. Not only that, but I guarantee you that Alice is making an attempt to get herself all prettied up to impress you, so don't make fun of her spa time. Instead, give her lots of compliments on how great her hair looks."

Mitch groaned. "I have a lot to learn."

"Yes, you do. But I'll help you. And since you're not doing anything at the moment, why don't we start lessons right now? I need to get this Christmas tree decorated. We can talk while I do that. I'll tell you about some of Alice's favorite things, and you can tell me what you know of Simon's murder case. Deal?"

Mitch smiled. "Deal. I might even help you hang a few ornaments."

"That's what I'm talking about!" I grinned as I went to start opening the first box of ornaments, and Mitch followed me.

"Unfortunately, I don't have that much to tell you," he said in a frustrated tone of voice. "We've analyzed all the evidence from the crime scene looking for DNA or fingerprints, but we weren't able to find anything conclusive. Whoever did this must have been careful to wear gloves while strangling poor Simon. And we haven't been able to find any other clues that point definitively to one suspect or the other."

"No?" I raised a questioning eyebrow. "I heard that the security footage Colleen gave you did show Lynette's dog tattoo."

Mitch nodded. "It did, and she's our most likely suspect at this point. She has no real alibi, for one thing. She says she was at home at the time of the murder, but there's no one who can verify that. And she does appear to have been the one who vandalized Simon's Christmas decorations. Still, the fact that she damaged his decorations isn't necessarily evidence that she killed him. It's a pretty big jump to go from destroying fake gingerbread men to strangling someone in cold blood. We need more evidence if we're going to charge her."

I frowned. "And I'm assuming it hasn't been easy to find any more evidence?"

"Exactly. No one seems to have seen or heard anything useful. There were quite a few people who disliked Simon, but so far no motives have emerged that seem strong enough for murder. I can tell you all about Simon's and Colleen's statements, if you want. Maybe you'll catch something one of them said that's helpful that I didn't catch. I'm at a complete loss, and Colleen can't seem to remember anything else about Vinny or Lynette that would make the case against them stronger."

I nodded, trying not to seem ridiculously overexcited by the fact that Mitch was going to tell me everything. It was possible that I wouldn't figure out anything more from the clues than he had, but it was worth a try. I wanted to review all of the evidence I possibly could. I gave Mitch a hopeful look, not wanting to push my luck too far, but feeling desperate to solve the case.

"Do you think I might be able to review the security footage Colleen gave you as well? Just to see if anything else sticks out to me about it other than Lynette's tattoo?"

Mitch nodded. "Sure. Why don't you come by the station tomorrow? I'll be there all day, so just come when you have time. Just to warn you, though: there isn't much interesting to see. It's just Lynette tossing around a bunch of Simon's Christmas decorations."

"I understand," I said as I started to pull some sparkling red ornaments out of the giant box of ornaments I'd purchased. "But I'd still like to take a look at it. You never know what might jump out at you."

"True enough. Here, hand me some of those ornaments and I'll start hanging some near the top for you."

I grinned and handed Mitch the box. "You are useful, after all."

He gave me a longsuffering look. "I'd say I've been quite useful today. Now, your turn to be useful. Tell me how I can win Alice over."

I grinned, and started to explain to him some of Alice's favorite restaurants, music, and activities. Mitch shouldn't have worried, though. I had a feeling that he could have taken Alice to a fast food restaurant and the two of them could have had a good time together. I'd never considered it before, but now that they'd started showing an interest in each other, it was obvious that they were the perfect match. Mitch's stubborn hardheadedness and Alice's sweet calm made them the perfect duo. Plus, the two of them were adorable together. They made one good-looking couple.

And hey, I wasn't going to complain if I got something out of all of this. I'm not sure I would have been able to get any information on Simon's murder from Mitch if not for the fact that he wanted information about Alice from me.

And I needed as much information as I could get. As I hung another Christmas ornament on my café's new tree, I could hear the clock, ticking toward Christmas.

I hoped that something Mitch was going to tell me would be more useful than he thought.

CHAPTER TWELVE

A little under two hours later, my tree was decorated beautifully, Mitch and I had finished the bottle of wine I'd opened, and I'd picked his brain to learn every detail I possibly could about Simon's murder case.

Unfortunately, there weren't that many details. Mitch hadn't been kidding when he'd said that the clues on the case were few and far between. He told me everything that Colleen had said, but none of it was news to me. His rundown of Lynette's and Vinny's statements was equally unenlightening, and I was beginning to think that he had agreed to let me work on the case not because he wanted information on Alice, but because he actually needed my help but didn't want to admit it.

Whatever his reasons, I was glad he was letting me in on the clues. And even though I was bummed that there wasn't more progress on the case already, I determined that I wasn't going to waste time wishing that things were different. I didn't have the luxury of whining right now. I needed to focus on solving things.

After Mitch left my café and I'd cleaned up the mess from our pie-eating and tree-decorating, I decided that I should visit Colleen. I certainly didn't want to push her to talk about Simon's murder if she wasn't ready to talk about it, but she seemed like the type that found talking therapeutic. If I could be a listening ear, I might make her feel better—and I might learn something useful about the case in the process. That sounded like a win-win to me.

Before I went anywhere, however, I was going to have to clean up a bit. I'd shaken most of the pine needles out of my hair by now, but my clothes were still covered in sap, and I was sure I had streaks of dirt on my face from the day's adventures. It was probably better if I headed home and dropped Sprinkles off, anyway. I wasn't sure that Colleen was a fan of dogs, and he was probably just going to have to wait outside if I took him.

After boxing up a cranberry vodka crumble to take to Colleen, I went home and cleaned up as best I could. The sap wasn't easy to get off of the spots where it had touched my hands and face, and I had a feeling it might never come out of my clothes. But at least after a hot shower I didn't look like I'd just finished fighting with a pine tree, which is essentially what had happened outside my café earlier.

I said a quick goodbye to Sprinkles, who seemed happy enough to curl up in his plush dog bed and take a nap. Usually, he didn't like it if I left him behind when I went sleuthing, but after the busy day we'd had, I guess he didn't mind the chance to chill out.

There would be no chilling out for me. I needed to get moving on this case, and every minute I waited was a minute more that the tourists were staying far away from Sunshine Springs.

The knowledge that I didn't have time to waste was the only thing that kept me going as I drove toward Colleen's house. I suddenly had doubts about whether this was a good idea. Would she really feel better if someone showed up at her house offering to talk, or was I just telling myself that so I didn't feel badly about bothering a new widow? As important as solving this case was to me, I didn't want to do so at the expense of Colleen's feelings. I decided that I would knock on her door and offer her the pie, but I would not be the first to mention anything about Simon. If she invited me in and wanted to talk, of course I would let her. But I would be very, very careful not to do anything to push her. For all I knew, I was wrong about the fact that she wanted to talk, and what she actually wanted was just to be left alone.

When I pulled up in front of Colleen's house, however, it became apparent that she did not want to be left alone. Or, if she did, no one was respecting those wishes. Her long driveway was full of cars, and there were also cars parked up and down her street. I had to park half a block away, and even then the spot I found was a tight fit.

Now, I was more unsure than ever over whether I should be here. Was I interrupting something? To my shame, I hadn't paid much attention to when Simon's funeral had been scheduled. Had it been today, and were all these people here to pay their respects?

I again almost turned around and went home, but then I decided that if people were paying respects, I might as well join them. I hadn't known Simon well, and, to be honest, he'd seemed like a bit of a jerk. But it was always sad when someone died, and I felt badly for Colleen and what she was going through. Since I was here, I should at least go drop off the pie I'd brought and offer my condolences.

I carefully carried the pie as I walked toward Colleen's house, and I felt a pang of sadness as I saw the elaborate Christmas decorations in her yard. There were spots that looked a little bare, where Simon had clearly been intending to add more decorations, and those spots would probably never be filled now. But the decorations that Simon had already put up looked incredible, and even though he hadn't seemed like the nicest person, I had to admit that he had a talent for creating a holiday wonderland. No wonder he'd won the decorating contest for several years running.

I frowned thinking about how Simon had been accused of cheating. If those allegations were true, then Simon hadn't deserved to win, no matter how much decorating talent he had. Of course, he hadn't deserved to die, either. I shook my head in bewilderment. People in this town took this contest a bit too seriously.

But my bewilderment only increased as I approached Colleen's front door. Loud, peppy holiday music drifted out into her front lawn—hardly the sort of thing you'd expect to be played after someone's funeral. It almost sounded like a lively Christmas party in there, but that couldn't be right. Surely, Colleen wasn't hosting a Christmas party days after Simon had died.

I timidly reached up and rang the doorbell, trying to peer through the frosted glass on the front door to see what was going on inside. I could see figures moving around, but everything was too blurry for me to make out who they were or what exactly they were doing.

After a full minute, I was still waiting for someone to answer the door. Impatiently, I rang the bell again. It was no wonder that no one had heard it. People were laughing and singing inside, and, from the way their blurry figures were moving around, it looked like they were dancing. If this was a post-funeral party, it was the strangest one I'd ever been too.

I rang the bell several times in succession, hoping that someone would hear it if it was going off over and over. That seemed to do the trick, because a few moments later Colleen herself swung the door wide open.

She was laughing, and had a wide smile on her face, which was almost as shocking as the outfit she was wearing. She wore a bright green dress that was studded with Christmas lights that lit up. She literally looked like a twinkling Christmas tree. Miniature red ornaments hung from her ears, and her hair was pulled up into a glamorous bun that had been sprayed over with some sort of glitter hairspray.

She definitely didn't look like a grieving widow, and the shock of seeing her in such festive attire with such a brilliant smile on her face left me a bit speechless.

She, however, was not speechless. Her eyes widened slightly at the sight of me, then she started laughing again. "Oh my, it's the pie lady, isn't it? Izzy, dear, what are you doing here? Surely you're not interested in attending a party with a bunch of women twice your age?"

"Uh…" I said, grasping for words. "I'm pretty sure you're not actually twice my age. But anyway, I had no idea you were having a party. I came to bring you pie and offer you condolences on Simon's death."

Colleen laughed, then hiccupped, and I realized that she was quite tipsy. Her speech slurred slightly as she spoke again. "Oh! Pie! How lovely. Do come in. We were just winding down the party, so you won't be bothering anyone. The white elephant gift exchange is already done."

Before I could say anything, Colleen grabbed my hand and pulled me into her house. The motion was so sudden and unexpected that I almost dropped the box of pie I held. I looked around at the other ladies in Colleen's house as she practically ran toward the kitchen, dragging me along. This party didn't look like it was winding down. Many of the women looked just as tipsy as Colleen, and most of them were dressed just as festively. Piles of wrapping paper littered the floor in the living room, presumably from the white elephant gift exchange, and I tried to reconcile everything I was seeing with the fact that I was in the home of a woman who had lost her husband to a brutal murder a few days ago. Ordinarily, a rambunctious Christmas party full of slightly toasted women wouldn't be so out of the ordinary in Sunshine Springs. But it didn't make sense when the woman hosting the party should be grieving, not celebrating. Something didn't seem right here, and I determined that I was going to get Colleen to talk. Forget about dancing around her feelings. She didn't seem to be all that worried about having space to grieve.

When we arrived in the kitchen, I was greeted by several more women who were sipping sparkling wine and sampling a wide variety of holiday treats.

"Look who I found!" Colleen said in a loud, sing-song voice. "Izzy, the pie lady! And she has pie!"

Colleen hiccupped, then giggled. And then she grabbed the pie box from me and shoved aside a plate of brownies to make room for the cranberry vodka crumble. The group in the kitchen squealed in delight, then descended upon the pie box like a pack of drunken vultures. I stood back and watched as they grabbed forks and dug right in, not even bothering with plates. Lots more hiccupping and giggling ensued, and all I could do was stare in amazement. There were plenty of other treats available, but my pie seemed to be the most wanted dessert of the moment. I should have felt a puff of pride, but I couldn't feel anything at the moment except shock. That shock must have shown on my face, because a few moments later, a woman was sidling up next to me and chuckling.

"They are quite enthusiastic, aren't they?"

I glanced over at the woman, whose face I recognized but whose name I didn't know. "Uh, yes. Quite."

The woman smiled and extended a slim hand to shake mine. "I'm Lucy. One of Colleen's friends and a regular at her annual White Elephant Gift Exchange."

Lucy seemed to be mercifully sober, and I jumped at the chance to ask someone who wasn't in a constant state of hiccups and giggles what all of this ruckus was about.

"I'm Izzy," I replied, although technically Colleen had already introduced me to the entire group. "I didn't realize Colleen had an annual party, although I must say I'm surprised to see her having such a lively party so soon after…"

I trailed off, feeling awkward mentioning Simon's death in the middle of such a happy atmosphere. But Lucy had no such qualms.

"So soon after Simon was murdered?" she finished for me. "Yes, I suppose it does seem a bit crass. But that's Colleen for you."

Lucy raised her shoulders in a slight shrug, as though that explained everything. But I was still confused, and now that I had Lucy talking, I intended to get some answers out of her.

"What do you mean, 'that's Colleen?' Is she generally a crass sort of person?" I raised a questioning eyebrow. The question was perhaps a bit bold, but I didn't have time to waste being timid. I had a murder case to solve and that meant I needed to learn everything possible about everyone involved. Colleen was acting so strangely that I couldn't help feeling like she was happy about Simon's passing, and that was worrisome. I couldn't imagine that she herself had had something to do with his untimely demise, but she certainly didn't seem to be worried about playing the part of a grieving widow.

"Colleen deals with bad days by having parties," Lucy explained. "She's a bit infamous for her parties. The White Elephant exchange is an annual affair, but when Colleen is in a bad mood she likes to throw a random party and get quite drunk. As you can imagine, she's been in quite a bad mood the last couple of days. This party was already planned, so rather than cancelling it, she decided to forge ahead and grieve in her own way, with a couple dozen of her closest friends."

I surveyed the room of giggling women. I could not imagine throwing a party days after a loved one had died, but I supposed we all grieved in our own ways.

Lucy chuckled, clearly seeing the doubt on my face. "I know it doesn't seem like the healthiest way to move on. But if you knew Colleen, you would know that this is how she copes."

"Well, I hope she's coping okay," I said doubtfully. I could only imagine how Colleen would feel the next morning, when she woke up with a horrible hangover and a husband who was still very dead.

Worries like that were the furthest thing from Colleen's mind at the moment, though. She looked up at me just then and grinned, then held her fork high in the air.

"Three cheers for the pie lady!" she slurred out merrily. The room erupted into chaotic cheering, and soon other women were drifting in from the living room to see what all the fuss was about. Unfortunately for them, the pie I'd brought in was almost completely gone. The drunken vultures had managed to demolish it in a matter of minutes. I found myself suddenly surrounded by a crowd of women begging me for more pie, as though I could magically produce one from my pocket.

"I'm sorry," I said, taking a step backward. "I would have brought more if I'd known there was a party going on. I was just trying to do something nice for Colleen after...the rough week she's had."

I wasn't sure whether mentioning Simon's death was the smart thing to do at the moment or not, but my comment about a rough week was clear enough for Colleen to latch onto the chance for a good rant. She waved her fork above her head in an even wilder motion, and I was a bit afraid that she was going to bring it down for emphasis and accidentally stab someone in the eye.

"It *has* been a rough week!" she declared, her formerly happy face darkening into furious storm clouds. "If it wasn't for all of you, I don't know how I would have made it through. I'm sure Simon is looking down on all of us right now and smiling. He knows how much I loved a good party, and I want to dedicate this party to his memory!"

The women cheered, and shouts of "To Simon!" rang out as they raised their glasses and then took long sips of their drinks. I watched the whole scene in confused fascination, wondering whether Simon really would be glad that such a wild party was being thrown just days after his murder.

Almost as if she could read my mind, Colleen pointed her fork in my direction and made a jabbing motion. "Simon would have wanted this!" she declared. "He would have wanted me to continue on living. Christmas was his favorite time of year, and he would have been happy to see me embracing the season even in his absence."

I nodded demurely, because what else could I do? And then, a moment later, Colleen burst into tears.

"Oh, how can I go through Christmas without him?" she wailed. "He loved the holidays so much. It's so cruel that I've lost him at what was the happiest time of the year for him."

The women surrounded her, giving her hugs and patting her on the back. Someone produced a box of tissues, and I felt horrible for ever questioning her motives for throwing the party. I'd lost my own parents unexpectedly in a car accident when I was younger, and I remembered feeling horribly frustrated when people tried to tell me the appropriate way to grieve. Everyone dealt with things differently, and if throwing her annual party in the face of tragedy was what she needed to do, then who was I to judge?

Beside me, Lucy shook her head and clucked her tongue

sympathetically. "It's all such a shame. I wasn't Simon's biggest fan, true. I thought he didn't appreciate Colleen and how amazing she is. But I still can't believe that someone would murder him! And over money! Can you imagine? How can anyone live with themselves after killing another human being over a thousand dollars?"

I glanced over at Lucy, wondering whether she might have any information that could point me in the right direction. She seemed quite knowledgeable about both Simon and Colleen, and I decided that if I was going to get anything useful out of this visit, then she might be my best bet.

"Do you have any idea who might have wanted that money badly enough to actually kill him?" I asked bluntly, keeping my voice low so that I didn't draw attention from the weeping Colleen or her crowd of supporters.

Lucy snorted. "It's obvious, isn't it? It was Lynette."

I couldn't keep a disappointed expression from crossing my face. It sounded like Lucy didn't have any new suspects to share with me. But Lucy noticed my face, and narrowed her eyes at me.

"I know Mitch and his little crew of detectives down at the police station don't think they have enough evidence to charge Lynette. But they need to open their eyes."

"Why do you say that?" I asked, my heart beating faster in my chest. Did Lucy have dirt on Lynette that Mitch had yet to hear about?

Lucy rolled her eyes, as though the answer should have been obvious. "Oh, come on. Everyone in town knows you're always sticking your nose in Mitch's murder cases, so I'm sure you've got the latest information on this one. I'm sure you've heard of the video footage Colleen has of Lynette in her yard, destroying Simon's decorations."

Another wave of disappointment washed over me. This was old news. "I have heard of it," I admitted. "But even though it makes Lynette look bad, it's not conclusive evidence. It's a big jump to go from destroying someone's fake Santa to strangling them with a pine garland."

Lucy waved a dismissive hand in my direction. "It is a jump, but not as big a jump as you make it seem. The two of them hated each other, and everyone knows it. Besides, everyone also knows how badly she needed money. It's obvious she was the one trying to blackmail Simon."

I perked up a bit at this. I hadn't heard anyone talking yet about how Lynette needed money. "I didn't know about that," I said. "What did she need money for?"

Lucy gave me an exasperated look. "Some detective you are. Have you even interrogated Lynette?"

"I've talked to her, but she didn't mention any financial problems."

"Well, of course she wouldn't mention them. But you should have been grilling her about her finances until she admitted the truth to you."

"Which is?"

"Which is that she was desperately trying to figure out a way to pay for surgery for that blasted dog of hers. The thing apparently has a tumor, which is going to be quite expensive to remove. Lynette could pay for it if just she sold off some of her things. Goodness knows her house is full enough of junk."

I was silent for a few moments, mulling over this information. I hadn't asked Lynette about her finances, although now that I thought about it, that would have been an obvious thing to do. I'd taken one look at her house and figured she had plenty of money to spare. But appearances could be deceiving, and it was no secret how much she adored her dog. She had the thing tattooed on her arm, after all!

Lucy was looking at me with a superior expression on her face. "I thought you were a bit more competent than Mitch, but I guess not. Sounds like you haven't done a very thorough job of investigating."

Suddenly, I wasn't as eager to talk to Lucy as I had been at the beginning of our conversation. I felt my cheeks heating up with anger, and I gave her an annoyed glare. "No, I haven't done a thorough job of investigating, because I'm not an official investigator. Yes, I've spent some time helping Mitch look into murder cases, but it's not my full-time job. I have a café to run, so I can't be expected to be a perfect detective."

Lucy shrugged and reached to grab a cookie from a nearby tray. "No need to get so defensive. I'm just saying that if Mitch or you or whoever is looking into this wants to actually make progress, then Lynette needs to be checked into again. Mitch doesn't seem interested in doing that."

"Mitch is a very good detective," I insisted, feeling the need to come to my friend's defense. "I bet that he *has* talked to Lynette about her finances, but the fact that she needed money in itself isn't proof that she murdered him."

"It's not definitive proof, but it gives her a motive."

"Sure, but tell me this: if Lynette was blackmailing Simon for money, why would she kill him? It doesn't make sense to strangle him if she needed a thousand dollars from him. It's not like he's going to win the decorating contest or give her the money when she's dead."

As I finished speaking, I suddenly realized that the room had gone terribly quiet. I gulped, looking up to see that everyone in the room was staring at Lynette and me. Colleen, in particular, was staring daggers at me.

"How can you defend Lynette?" she spat out at me, her voice seething. Her cheeks were still wet from tears, but she had stopped crying for the moment. Instead of wailing, she was directing her energy at reprimanding me. I gulped again, unsure of the best way to handle this incredibly awkward situation.

"It's not that I'm defending her," I tried to explain. "I'm just saying that for Mitch to charge her, he needs to gather more evidence. He's trying to do that, but it's a process that takes time."

Colleen crossed her arms. "It wouldn't take so much time if he would pay attention to what's right in front of him. Lynette hated Simon so much that she was willing to blackmail him. Something must have gone wrong when they met. Obviously, no one knows exactly how things played out, but it seems pretty obvious to me that Lynette found out she wasn't going to get her money. My guess is that Simon refused to give it to her, because he knew she had no basis to accuse him of cheating. That must have made Lynette so angry that she lost control and strangled him."

"It does sound like a plausible theory," I said soothingly. I didn't want to get Colleen any more riled up than she already was, but in truth her explanation didn't make perfect sense. From what I'd heard, Simon had indeed cheated. Perhaps Colleen didn't know, or perhaps she didn't want to admit the truth of that even to herself, but from what Vinny had told me it was a pretty clear instance of Simon breaking the rules of the decorating contest. Not only that, but was it really possible for Lynette to overpower Simon and strangle him? I wasn't sure she was strong enough to do that, although I supposed it was possible if she caught him by surprise.

But on the whole, Vinny seemed a much likelier suspect than Lynette. He also hated Simon, and he actually had the strength to overpower Simon easily. Not only that, but Theo and I had spotted him fighting with Simon right before Simon's murder. If you asked me, it sounded like Vinny had been the one to lose control and kill Simon. I wasn't going to say any of that to Colleen right now, though. Not when she was looking at me with so much venom in her eyes, and spewing accusations against Lynette.

"I know this is upsetting, and I'm so sorry you're going through it," I said. "But Mitch is a good detective, and I promise he'll get to the bottom of things. If there's more evidence to find on Lynette, he *will* find it."

"He doesn't need more evidence. He just needs to arrest her." Colleen waved her fork around wildly as she spoke, then downed another half glass of champagne in one quick series of giant gulps.

I decided that it was time for me to make my exit. Colleen was only getting drunker by the moment, and talk of Lynette was only upsetting her. I had a feeling I wasn't going to learn anything further, and I was only going to make Colleen angry at me. Besides, I'd already learned one interesting piece of information: the fact that Lynette had needed money did make her look guiltier. Admittedly, I felt like a fool for not trying to look into her finances more than I had. I had assumed she was well enough off that she didn't need the money, but assumptions don't make for good detective work.

I wasn't going to make that mistake again. I wasn't going to assume anything—including the fact that Lynette had been the one to vandalize Simon's decorations. I didn't care that Mitch had already looked at the security footage, and that everyone else insisted the vandal had been Lynette. I needed to go view the security footage with my own two eyes. No more assumptions.

I bid Colleen goodbye as quickly as I could, offering my condolences and telling her to feel free to stop by the café anytime she wanted more pie, on the house. Even as I walked away from the kitchen, Colleen's sobs were growing louder. I shook my head, again questioning the wisdom of her holding such a big party just days after losing her spouse. It didn't seem like the best way to grieve, but again, it wasn't my place to judge.

Colleen could grieve in whatever way she felt best, and I would focus my attention on figuring out who killed her husband. As I walked back to my car, I picked up my phone to call Mitch. I wanted to make sure that I could get in to see the footage from Colleen's security camera as soon as possible. So much of the talk about the case had centered around that footage. I had a gut instinct that if I could just view that footage, I would find a new clue that would help me unravel this case.

I prayed with all my might that my gut instinct was right. The clock was ticking on Christmas, and I wasn't going to let Sunshine Springs down.

CHAPTER THIRTEEN

Early the next evening, I sat in one of the interrogation rooms at the police station, watching the security footage and thinking that my gut instinct had been very wrong. There was nothing exciting to see on the black-and-white video of the vandal destroying Simon's decorations. Whoever was causing the destruction was wearing oversized black sweats and a black ski mask, making it impossible to tell who they were. The sweats were so baggy that I couldn't have even said for sure whether whoever was hiding underneath them was skinny or not. The vandal had taken great care to hide their true identity.

I tried to keep an open mind as I watched Santa and his reindeer toppling over as the vandal whacked at them with a giant statue of a lollipop that had been part of a glittering gingerbread house moments before. There must be some clue here I was missing. I just wasn't looking closely enough.

But as the vandal finished his or her work and started walking away from the decorations, I was still at a loss. I hadn't seen anything useful, and the counter on the video was nearing zero, showing that the footage was almost over.

"Here," Mitch said, pointing his pen in the direction of the screen. "This is where you can see the tattoo."

I leaned forward to watch closely as the vandal walked very close to where the camera was hidden on Simon and Colleen's front porch. The vandal paused, and turned as though surveying his or her work. Then the vandal pushed the sleeves of the baggy sweatshirt up to his or her elbows.

When the sweatshirt's sleeves were pulled up, the camera showed an unobstructed view of a tattoo of a dog that looked exactly like Lynette's tattoo. Mitch quickly paused the video so I could take a moment to look carefully at the design, and I nodded slowly, affirming that it was definitely

Lynette's dog. Then, even though I'd already been told that I'd be seeing this, I let out a long sigh.

Was I sighing in frustration, or relief? I wasn't sure. I suppose I'd been hoping that somehow everyone had been mistaken, and that the vandal wouldn't turn out to be Lynette. Vinny, with his abrasive personality and crusading craziness, seemed so much likelier to murder someone. But the tattoo on the screen in front of me was undeniably Lynette's. Even though the footage was black and white, and not exactly crystal-clear, it wasn't horribly grainy either. I was definitely staring at an inked-on likeness of Lynette's dog.

"Funny, isn't it?" Mitch mused. "She took such great care to dress in baggy clothes and a ski mask to hide her identity. Then, at the very end, she ruins her cover by showing that tattoo for a few seconds. You'd think she'd know better."

I nodded glumly as Mitch hit play again, and Lynette pulled down her sweatshirt sleeves once more, then walked away. A few moments later, the footage came to an end. I remained silent, staring at the blank screen and trying to figure out where to go from here. Another day had passed, and I still hadn't discovered anything new. At what point was I going to have to admit that my first holiday season in Sunshine Springs had been completely ruined?

"Still doesn't prove anything, of course," Mitch said, restating what both of us already knew. "Just because she vandalized Simon's decorations doesn't mean she killed him. But it does make her look guilty."

I nodded, not paying very close attention to what he was saying. Something about the footage was still bothering me. I had a deep conviction that I was missing an important clue here, but what was it?

Then, suddenly, it hit me. I sat straight up in my chair, my eyes wide.

"Wait a minute. Rewind that footage for a minute or so. Go back to the point right before Lynette walked over to stand directly in front of the security camera."

Mitch gave me a curious look, but shrugged and did as I asked. Once again, we watched closely as Lynette finished smashing Simon's decorations, then walked away from them, pausing right in front of the camera. Again, I saw her make the mistake of pushing up her sleeves to reveal the tattoo before walking off.

Only I wasn't so sure it had been a mistake.

"I don't think that's Lynette," I said, finally tearing my eyes away from the projector screen to look at Mitch. Predictably, he looked at me like I'd completely lost my mind.

"Izzy, didn't you see the tattoo? No one else has a tattoo like that."

"Exactly. So if she shows her tattoo, everyone is going to know it was her on the lawn, right?"

"Well, yes. That's the whole point of Colleen showing me this footage. To prove that Lynette was on their property, destroying their decorations."

I shook my head. "Think about it, Mitch. Why would she go to so much trouble to dress head to toe in black, but then at the last moment push up her sleeves to reveal her most unique identifying characteristic? Not only that, but why would she walk up to the porch, right in front of the camera, instead of walking away?"

Mitch frowned. "I'm not sure I'm following you."

I jumped up and started excitedly pacing back and forth across the room. "If this vandal was Lynette, it would have made sense for her to walk off the property and leave quickly when she was done with her little rampage. But she didn't. She walked closer to the house and stood right in front of the camera, pushed her sleeve up to reveal the tattoo that would tell everyone who she was, and only then did she walk back in the opposite direction to actually leave."

Mitch was still frowning at me. "Well, I'm sure she didn't realize that there happened to be a camera right where she paused."

"Maybe Lynette doesn't know about the camera. But the person impersonating her obviously did. They walked right up to it on purpose and rolled up their sleeves to reveal the tattoo, ensuring that when the footage was reviewed everyone would think it was Lynette."

Mitch shook his head slowly. "It's an interesting theory, I'll give you that. But there's just one little problem: Lynette's tattoo is very detailed and intricate. It's not something that could be easily replicated, and even if it was, it would be pretty obvious. It's not like you can just wash a tattoo off, so anyone crazy enough to get a matching tattoo would have to hide their wrist for pretty much the rest of their life if they didn't want to be discovered."

"Well, yes, if it was a real tattoo. But it would be easy enough to draw on a fake tattoo if you had a photo of the original to work from. That camera is decent quality, but it's not like it's HD ten million or whatever the top quality level is these days."

Mitch chuckled at that. "No, the camera is definitely not HD ten million. But I still find it hard to believe that someone could replicate that tattoo. That's a lot of trouble to go to just to frame Lynette for knocking over a couple of reindeer."

"If it was just the reindeer, I'd agree. But this isn't just about the reindeer. It's about Simon's murder. Someone was planning to murder him, and they thought that planting evidence against Lynette would be the best way to cast suspicion away from them."

Mitch pondered this for a few moments. "I guess that's possible, but it still seems a tad bit farfetched."

I was getting annoyed with him. "This is about a murder case, Mitch!

Someone planning a murder knows that if they're caught they're pretty much going to jail for life, or worse. I think they'd go to great lengths to avoid that, don't you?"

Mitch nodded, but he still looked doubtful. "It's an interesting theory. But tell me, Miss Detective, *who* do you think would do this? Vinny?"

"Maybe," I said. "He definitely wasn't a fan of Simon, and he speaks of Lynette like she's the devil incarnate. But I have this weird feeling that we're missing someone here. Who else needed money? Who else didn't like Simon?"

Mitch snorted. "A better question might be who *did* like Simon. He wasn't exactly a town favorite. In fact, earlier today I was having coffee at Alice's café and Stuart was ranting about Simon. Several people tried to quiet him down, telling him that it was bad karma to speak ill of the dead, but he didn't seem to care. He continued right on with his tirade."

I stopped my pacing and stared at Mitch. Why hadn't I seen this before? Stuart, as nice as he was, was definitely connected to this case. He'd had trouble with Vinny, and he'd seemed to know a lot about both Lynette and Simon when I'd talked to him the day I bought the Christmas tree for my café. Not only that, but he was definitely hurting for money. He'd told me how the Christmas curse boycott was hurting him, but he'd also explained that he'd been hurting for money even before then. He'd had a difficult couple of years, he'd said.

I narrowed my eyes at Mitch. "What exactly did Stuart say?"

"Oh, it was mostly just a long rant about how Simon was a cheater, both in life and in the decorating contest. I guess Vinny told him that Simon had cheated on the decorating contest, but Stuart said Simon had also cheated him out of payment for a special order of Christmas trees."

My heart was pounding in my chest. It sounded like Stuart had definitely needed money. I didn't want to believe that the sweet old man who owned the Sunshine Springs Christmas Tree farm had murdered Simon, but it sounded like he'd hated Simon and had motive. "Did he say anything else about the Christmas tree order?"

Mitch furrowed his brow as he tried to remember. "He said that Simon had special ordered some artificial trees that were in various 'candy' colors. I guess Stuart doesn't normally sell artificial trees, but he can get them at a good wholesale price if he needs to. Simon asked him for a special deal on them and Stuart agreed, because even though it was only a tiny bit of profit, profit is profit. After the trees arrived and Stuart delivered them to Simon's yard, Simon promised to send a check with payment for the trees. Stuart agreed because he couldn't imagine that anyone in Sunshine Springs, even Simon, would default on payment to another Sunshine Springs local."

"But Simon never sent the payment," I guessed.

Mitch nodded. "Exactly. Simon never paid, and when Stuart tried to get him to send the payment, Simon simply said he could sue him for the money if he wanted to. But of course, the cost of a suit, even in small claims court, would be more trouble than it was worth for such a small amount."

Everything was becoming clear. "It must have been Stuart," I said, starting to pace again.

But Mitch wasn't so convinced. In fact, he seemed surprised by the accusation. "Look, you asked me who else hated Simon, and Stuart is one example. But he's far from the only one. The more I look into this case, the more I'm realizing that Simon had screwed over almost everyone in town in one way or another. My point was that merely hating Simon isn't in itself enough for me to think someone murdered him."

"But it was more than just hatred with Stuart," I pointed out. "He also had a money motive. His Christmas tree business hasn't been doing well, and then Simon defaulted on a payment that I'm sure Stuart really needed. It makes perfect sense. Stuart would have been happy to go destroy Simon's decorations, including many of the trees Simon had bought from him but never paid for. Because Vinny was always around the tree farm, Stuart knew all about the drama between Lynette and Simon. Vinny hated Simon, too, so he spent a good deal of his time railing against him. Stuart would have known that framing Lynette for the destruction of the decorations would make perfect sense. He must have tried to blackmail Simon for the money he was owed, and then somewhere along the line the blackmail scheme exploded and Stuart ended up killing Simon. All the pieces fit."

"All the pieces except the fact that Stuart has been one of Sunshine Springs most upstanding residents for decades, as was his father before him. I find it hard to believe that he would do any of these things— vandalism, blackmail, or especially murder."

I sat down again, this time taking a seat directly across the table from Mitch. "I agree that he doesn't seem like the murdering type, and you know him much better than I do. But you can't write him off just because he's nice. We've seen again and again that people who don't seem like they could possibly be criminals turn out to be the worst criminals of all."

Mitch sighed, then looked up at the ceiling and cracked his knuckles. The sound used to bother me, but now I found it almost endearing. I knew it meant he was either troubled or excited about something, and I was hoping that this time it was a little bit of both. Sure, he might be troubled by the idea that Stuart had murdered someone, but perhaps he was a tiny bit excited, too. Perhaps we had just solved this case.

But when he looked back at me, I could see that he wasn't excited at all. He looked weary and frustrated. "I don't think he did it, honestly. But your theory does have some plausibility, so I'll at least talk to him."

I nodded. I couldn't ask for much more than that. We sat in silence for a few moments, as there didn't seem to be anything else to say about the case at the moment. Then, Mitch's phone buzzed, breaking the silence. He looked down at it, and I saw him grin.

"Let me guess," I said. "It's Alice?"

He shrugged sheepishly. "I don't hide my feelings very well, do I?"

"No, but that's okay. No need to hide them. If you care about her then you should feel free to shout it from the rooftops. She's a good woman."

"That she is. Look, I hate to rush you, but I'm supposed to be taking Alice out for dinner in a bit, and I'd like to have time to go home and freshen up a bit beforehand."

I grinned and raised my hands. "Say no more. I'll get out of your hair so you can get going. I need to go pick up Sprinkles from Grams' house, anyway. She's been watching him all day, and while I'm sure she'd love to keep him even longer, I'm scared to think of how much sugar he's been getting lately. I think the only thing Grams loves more than holiday baking is sharing what she bakes with her granddoggy."

I rolled my eyes, but Mitch only laughed. "Your Grams is a character, that's for sure. Tell her hello for me."

"Will do. And you make sure you talk to Stuart tomorrow," I said sternly.

Mitch raised his hands in a gesture of surrender. "I will, I will. I really don't think he's the murderer, so I wouldn't get your hopes up if I were you. But I'll at least talk to him."

I nodded and gave Mitch a quick goodbye hug before heading out to get Sprinkles. But despite what Mitch had said, I couldn't help feeling excited about the latest developments in the case. Perhaps Stuart was an unlikely suspect, but my theory made perfect sense. With any luck, this case would be solved tomorrow.

I couldn't help giving the air a little victory pump as I drove toward Grams. I was going to have a hard time sleeping tonight, because I could hardly wait to see what news Mitch would have for me about the case tomorrow.

CHAPTER FOURTEEN

After picking up Sprinkles, I felt too excited to go home. I had a feeling that Simon's murder case was on the verge of being solved, and I couldn't stand the idea of sitting around at my house, waiting for something to happen. I needed to calm down a bit, and the one person who could always help me make sense out of chaos was my best friend, Molly.

I headed to the library without bothering to text and ask if she was there. The library was on the way home, so I wouldn't be going out of my way if I stopped, and I thought it would be fun to surprise her if she was there. To my surprise, when I got there, not only was Molly's car in the parking lot, but Scott's and Theo's were as well.

I parked next to Theo's brand new sleek black Mercedes, and went inside, leaving Sprinkles to wait just outside the door. Molly loved my Dalmatian, but the library had a strict "no pets" rule. Sprinkles was used to this, and flopped dejectedly in his favorite grassy spot next to a small but well-tended garden in front of the library. Even now, in the middle of winter, the library staff had managed to keep a healthy amount of greenery growing in that garden. The mild Northern California weather made it possible to keep the garden up quite well even in December, and I smiled as I passed it. The beautiful plants always made me feel calmer, which was saying quite a bit at the moment. Things with Simon's murder case had me stressing out much more than was healthy, but I reminded myself that at least some progress had been made today, and that was a good thing.

When I walked into the library, the place was fairly empty. That wasn't all that surprising since it was only about fifteen minutes until closing time. There might be a few stragglers here and there, but almost everyone would have gone home by now.

The front desk, however, was not empty at all. Molly sat behind the desk, while Theo and Scott leaned on the counter, talking and laughing. All three of them were eating Chinese food from a trio of takeout boxes.

"Hey!" I said, trying to make my voice sound stern. "What's this? Did you all decide to have a party and not invite me?"

They all looked up in surprise, then grinned when they saw me. No one was fooled by my attempt to appear angry.

"Izzy!" Molly exclaimed. "Scott and Theo were hanging out at the winery because things have been so slow for both wine sales and package delivery. I convinced them to come by and bring me dinner, but I didn't call you because you've been so crazy busy! What are you up to now? I thought I wasn't going to get to see you again this week."

I walked up to the counter and swiped a fortune cookie from the corner of Theo's takeout box.

"Hey!" he protested. "That's my fortune."

"It's mine now," I told him in a saucy tone. Then I turned to Molly. "I've been trying to find clues on Simon's murder case, and I've been coming up short. But that all changed today."

"Really?" Scott asked, leaning in with interest. He was one of the top gossips of the town, so he thrived on the chance to hear juicy news before anyone else in Sunshine Springs.

I grinned at him. "Really. I've been so frustrated, so it was a big relief to finally make some progress. And you're never going to believe what I discovered."

I glanced around quickly to make sure no one else in the library was close enough to hear what I was saying, and then I quickly told them everything I'd learned about Simon's murder case since I last saw them. All three of my friends listened eagerly as I told them about Colleen's strange party and how I had learned of Lynette's supposed money troubles while there. Then, they widened their eyes in shock as I explained how I'd watched the footage from Colleen's security camera and realized that the tattoo on the vandal must have been a fake. But when I started to explain why I thought Stuart was the vandal, Molly started slowly shaking her head.

"I don't think so, Izzy," she said slowly. "I think your theory about the tattoo being an attempt to frame Lynette is correct, but I don't think that Stuart is your culprit."

I frowned in her direction. "Don't tell me you're going to defend Stuart just because he's a nice guy. That's basically what Mitch did."

Molly shrugged. "Stuart is a nice guy, but that's not why I'm defending him. I'm defending him because I'm pretty sure Vinny is the one who faked the tattoo."

Now I was intrigued. Molly rarely disagreed with me when I thought I'd figured out a clue on a murder case, so she must have had a good reason. "Why do you say that?" I asked.

Molly looked around to make sure no one else was listening, then she leaned in and spoke in a voice that was barely more than a whisper. "Because Vinny has been spending a lot of time at the library lately. A few weeks ago he checked out several books about learning to draw, as well as several books on the artistry of tattoos."

I blinked a few times, feeling a bit shocked at this information. "Wow."

Molly nodded. "'Wow', is right. I thought it was a bit strange, since Vinny doesn't strike me as the artist type. But I figured maybe he wanted to learn a new skill. I remember thinking that it would be good if he found a hobby besides harassing everyone over how much they're killing the environment."

"Except he wasn't trying to learn a new skill," Scott said. "He was trying to frame Lynette for his destruction of Simon's property."

"Exactly," Molly said. "And perhaps for Simon's murder as well?"

I shook my head, feeling a bit shell-shocked. I'd been so ready to blame Stuart for everything, but Mitch's instincts seemed to have been correct. If Vinny had gone to so much trouble to frame Lynette, then it wasn't a big leap to think that he'd gone to a lot of trouble to make the blackmail note and kill Simon. It still didn't make sense to me why someone would bother asking for money and then kill the very person they wanted money from, but I had seen Vinny's temper in action on multiple occasions. I could easily picture him getting so angry at Simon that he forgot all about the money and decided to strangle him instead.

I shoved the fortune cookie I was still holding into the pocket of my hoodie without opening it, ignoring Theo's glare. He was still annoyed that I'd stolen his cookie, but I had bigger things to worry about at the moment. "I have to call Mitch!"

I pulled my cell phone out of my other pocket and dialed Mitch's cell number, but he didn't answer. With a sigh, I dialed the police station instead. In the past, I'd insisted on speaking directly to Mitch instead of calling information in to the station, and that had nearly gotten me killed. This time, I wasn't going to wait to inform the police of what I knew. Not with a murderer on the loose. As much as I would have preferred to speak to Mitch directly, I didn't want to take a chance on Vinny somehow realizing I was onto him and getting away.

I wasn't sure there would be anyone at the station, since it was well past five p.m., but I had to try. The receptionist had surely gone home, but sometimes when the police department was in the middle of a big case, like a murder investigation, Mitch kept an officer at the station to man the phones, just in case.

"Sunshine Springs Police Station."

My heart leapt when the line was picked up on the second ring. I breathed a silent prayer of thanks that I was lucky enough to get a hold of someone without having to go through the dramatics of dialing 911. I didn't think this situation necessarily warranted use of an emergency line, but it wasn't something I wanted to wait until morning to tell the police about. The officer who answered the phone sounded extraordinarily bored, but his night was about to get a whole lot more interesting.

"This is Izzy James," I said excitedly. I felt a bit out of breath even though I was standing still. "Is Mitch around by chance?"

"No," the officer said, clearly stifling a yawn. "He left a while ago to take Alice to dinner. You know they're a couple now, right?"

"Yes, I know," I said impatiently. "Everyone in Sunshine Springs knows that. Are you the officer on duty?"

"Yeah," the officer said, then continued talking about Mitch and Alice as though that was the most exciting news of the week. "I didn't know Mitch had a soft spot for Alice until tonight. I'm always the last one to know everything! The only reason I found out was that Mitch asked me to call Alice and let her know that he was going to be late. He had to leave in a rush for an emergency. We're so short-staffed these days. Smith is on vacation. He went to visit his mother on the east coast for the Christmas holidays. Did you know he grew up in Boston? I never would have guessed. He doesn't have an accent at all."

"I don't care about where Smith is from! I have news about Simon's murder case! Do you think Mitch will be available to speak soon, or should I just have you take a report."

The officer sighed, clearly not happy with the idea of having to do the work of taking down a report. "I don't know, honestly. He was responding to reports of vandalism at Lynette's house. Her Christmas decorations were all being destroyed. Seems we have a Grinch of a vandal on the loose. Hopefully Lynette doesn't end up dead soon. Simon was killed right after his decorations were destroyed. Of course, Lynette is the one who destroyed Simon's decorations, so I have no clue who is destroying hers. Such a strange holiday season this year, don't you think?"

I was about to tell the officer to cut it with the rambling analysis and contact Mitch to tell him that Vinny was the murderer. Everything was falling into place: Vinny had been the one to vandalize Simon's yard, and had then killed Simon in a fit of rage. Now, Vinny was vandalizing Lynette's yard as well. It was no secret that he hated both Simon and Lynette. Was Lynette going to end up murdered soon as well? I gulped back a bubble of fear rising in my throat and opened my mouth to say that Mitch needed to be warned about Vinny and how dangerous he was. But before I could say anything, the door to the library burst open and Alice ran in, crying hysterically.

My jaw dropped in shock, and I nearly dropped my phone. Dread filled me as I looked at her distraught, tear-streaked face. "Alice? What's the matter?"

"Mitch was in a car wreck!" she shrieked. She said a bunch of other words, but I couldn't make them out between her hysterics. Theo, Molly and Scott all looked at Alice in alarm.

"What?" Theo roared. "What happened? Is he hurt?"

Theo's outburst only made Alice cry harder, and I glared at him. "You're not helping," I admonished, although I couldn't be too angry. Mitch was his best friend, so of course this news was upsetting. But if we wanted to figure out what was going on, we had to calm Alice down enough to talk. I stepped over to her and put my arm around her, speaking in a soothing tone. "Alice, take a few deep breaths and calm down. Tell us what happened so we can help."

Alice sniffed and nodded. "I was on my way to the restaurant where Mitch and I were going to have dinner tonight. He got caught up with work, so I was going to meet him there to save time. I was just driving past the library here when I heard on my police scanner that he'd been in a wreck! He was chasing down Vinny, and somehow Vinny's car collided with his!"

"You have a police scanner?" Scott asked in a confused voice.

"Mitch was chasing Vinny?" Theo asked at the same time.

Alice was sobbing again, so I took the opportunity to quickly explain what the officer at the police station had just told me on the phone. I realized then that I'd never actually finished the call with the officer, but when I glanced down at my phone, the call had ended. No surprise there. The officer had probably used the fact that I wasn't talking to him as an excuse to hang up and avoid having to do the work of a report.

Theo, Scott and Molly were a bit shocked by the news I'd just given them, and for a moment they stared at me in silence as Alice continued to sob.

"So let me get this straight," Theo said, his voice on edge. I could tell he was trying to remain calm, but it wasn't easy for him. "Mitch responded to a call of vandalism at Lynette's house, which must have turned out to be Vinny. Then Mitch was chasing down Vinny, and that chase ended in a wreck?"

"And Alice who for some reason has a police scanner heard about it," Scott finished, looking at Alice in hopes that she would explain more. She didn't, so he quickly prompted her. "Do you know if he's alright?"

"I don't know," she wailed. "On the scanner they said that Vinny ran him off the road, and then drove off. An ambulance was being called and I want to go see him but I'm crying too hard to drive straight right now."

"Yeah, you definitely shouldn't be driving," I said. "We don't want you to end up in a wreck as well."

"I can drive you there," Molly said. "I'll have my junior librarian close up the library."

"I'll come with you," Scott said. "Maybe there's some way I can help."

"I'm definitely not being left behind," Theo said, slamming his fist on the counter. "If Vinny hurt Mitch, he's going to pay for it!"

"Well, I'm not going to sit around here waiting for some news," I said. "Sounds like we're all going."

"Then let's go!" Theo said, already running toward the door. I ran after him, with Molly's voice behind me shouting across the library to her junior librarian that she was leaving for an emergency. I guess that was one instance where yelling in the library was okay.

Sprinkles was waiting just outside the door, standing tall at high alert. He must have seen Alice running in and known something was wrong.

"Come on, boy," I said. "We've got some work to do."

He ran after me and hopped in the backseat of Theo's Mercedes. I winced, hoping he didn't have muddy paws right now. Luckily, Theo loved dogs, and probably wouldn't be too angry if there were a few paw prints to clean off of his backseat.

Alice had parked right next to Theo, and I quickly helped Scott get a very hysterical Alice into her car and buckled in. The police scanner was still squawking, and it sounded like all available units were being dispatched to search for Vinny.

"Why *does* she have a police scanner?" Scott asked, apparently quite confused by the notion of the police chief's girlfriend having a scanner.

"She got it last month, when she was accused of murder," I explained as I double checked Alice's buckle. "She was trying to stay ahead of any police officers who might be chasing her down. I guess after she was cleared of murder she decided to keep the scanner to keep tabs on Mitch. She's a perpetual worrywart, so it must make her feel better to be able to check in and hear that he's okay."

Scott frowned as Molly ran out of the library toward Alice's car. "I guess that plan wasn't so great, since now she's actually heard bad news about him."

I let out an exasperated breath. "Well, the only thing to do now is go check on him. I hope he's alright."

Scott nodded and headed for the driver's seat of Alice's car. "See you at the crash site."

I nodded, then hopped into the passenger seat of Theo's car. Theo, who was already sitting impatiently in the driver's seat with the engine running, peeled out of his parking spot the second my passenger side door was closed.

"No one messes with my best friend," he growled as I struggled to buckle my seatbelt. "Let's roll."

And roll we did, at top speed. I held on for dear life and prayed that Mitch was going to be okay.

CHAPTER FIFTEEN

We arrived at the crash site well ahead of the others. Alice's sensible sedan had nothing on Theo's sporty Mercedes, and I doubted that Scott was driving like a racing star like Theo had. Alice had told us the location of the crash, but it would have been easy enough to find. The wreck had happened on a main thoroughfare through Sunshine Springs, and there were flashing lights everywhere. A police car, two fire trucks, and an ambulance were on the scene.

My heart sank as I saw Mitch's crushed squad car. The whole front driver's side was crumpled from where it had made contact with a large pole. Shattered glass littered the scene, sparkling red and blue from the emergency lights rotating overhead. It didn't look good for Mitch.

Theo squealed to a stop, and had barely put the car in park before he was bolting from his seat and sprinting toward the wreckage. I followed right after him, yelling over my shoulder to Sprinkles that he shouldn't run through the broken glass. The wrecked car was empty when we got to it, and I saw that the driver's side door had been completely removed. It looked like they'd had some trouble getting Mitch out.

Frantically, Theo and I both looked around, searching for Mitch's whereabouts. I just wanted to know that he was alive and okay. A moment later, Theo started running toward the ambulance and I followed him blindly. Sprinkles raced after us, barking at the top of his lungs.

There on a stretcher just outside the waiting ambulance, Mitch lay. Paramedics swarmed around him, placing a brace on his neck and one of his legs, I put my hand over my mouth to stifle back a cry, but Theo didn't bother acting tough.

"Mitch!" he exclaimed, tears rushing to his eyes as he tried to push his way through the paramedics to his best friend.

"Theo," Mitch rasped out. "You gotta let these guys do their work."

Theo looked only mildly apologetic as he stepped ever so slightly to the left to make room for the paramedics. "I was so worried," he choked out. "I heard you'd been in a crash, and when I saw your car over there, I feared the worst."

"I'm alright," Mitch said. "Leg's broken and I've got quite a few nasty cuts. Gonna have to get a few sets of stitches. But things could have been a lot worse."

"Is your neck okay?" I asked, speaking up for the first time. I eyed the neck brace warily, fearing that Mitch was in shock and didn't fully realize how serious his injuries were.

"Neck's fine. The brace is just a precaution." A smile crossed Mitch's face. "Good to see you, Izzy. Turns out Vinny is our vandal. You were right about the fake tattoo theory, but wrong about the culprit."

"I know," I said despondently. "I tried to warn you, but I was too late."

"It's alright. At least we know now. My boys will catch Vinny and he'll have to answer for all his crimes."

"Alright!" one of the paramedics called out. "Out of the way, folks. We gotta get Mitch into the ambulance and to the hospital."

"Wait," Mitch said. "Can one of you call Alice and let her know? We were supposed to be getting dinner."

I winced. "She already knows. She's the one who told us, actually. She heard it on the police scanner."

Mitch groaned. "Of course. I wish she'd get rid of that thing."

"She's on her way here, too," I said. "I'll let her know that you're mostly okay."

But before the paramedics could start loading Mitch into the ambulance, Alice was running up to the stretcher, sobbing out Mitch's name. I looked up to see Scott and Molly following behind her.

"Ma'am, we have to take him to the hospital. You can visit with him there," the exasperated paramedic explained.

"I'm not leaving him!" Alice cried out, rushing to Mitch's side and bending over to place a gentle kiss on his forehead. "I'll ride in the ambulance with him."

"I'm sorry, but only family members are allowed in the ambulance," the paramedic said apologetically.

"I'm not leaving him!" Alice declared, putting a hand on her hip and looking fiercer than I'd ever seen her as she stared down each of the paramedics in turn. Her eyes dared them to disagree with her.

Mitch chuckled. "Why don't you boys let her ride with me? She's the closest thing to family I've got, and I reckon one day soon enough she and I will actually be family."

Alice's jaw dropped at Mitch's words, and the rest of us all grinned from ear to ear. If I wasn't mistaken, Mitch had just hinted that there would be a proposal coming Alice's way in the not-too-distant future. I shook my head in amusement. Relationships sure did seem to move quickly here in Sunshine Springs. I supposed that was to be expected when most of the locals had known each other their whole lives.

The paramedic sighed, but couldn't hold back a small smile himself. "Fine. If it's alright with you, Sheriff, we'll let Alice ride along."

"It's more than alright with me," Mitch replied. "And the rest of you stay out of trouble."

He shook a warning finger at us, and we all did our best to look innocent as he was lifted into the ambulance and Alice climbed in after him. As soon as the ambulance sped away, Theo turned to look at us with a determined expression on his face.

"Are you guys thinking what I'm thinking?" he asked.

"That depends," I said, crossing my arms. "Are you thinking that there's no way you're going to stand around and do nothing while the criminal who almost killed Mitch is still on the loose?"

"Bingo," Theo said. "No offense to the Sunshine Springs Police Department, but I'm not leaving it up to them to catch Vinny. Not when I nearly lost my best friend tonight. Who wants to go on a little manhunt with me?"

I raised my hand, as did both Scott and Molly. Sprinkles barked his approval of our plan, and Theo nodded approvingly.

"Let's get to it, then. Time to go chase down Vinny Herron and show him that he messed with the wrong crew."

CHAPTER SIXTEEN

Theo's car was a bit of a tight fit for four adults plus a large Dalmatian, but we made it work. I sat in the front passenger seat, and Molly and Scott sat in the backseat with Sprinkles sandwiched between them. No matter how many times I told my stubborn pup to sit still, he kept leaning forward and sticking his head in the front between Theo and me. He was not going to miss a single moment of this adventure.

The big question of the moment was where, exactly, the adventure would take us. Theo started driving down the road in the direction Vinny had allegedly fled, but it had been quite some time since the crash had occurred. Vinny could be anywhere by now, and our initial enthusiasm for catching him was quickly tempered by the realization that we had no idea where to start.

"Tell you what," I said, finally landing on an idea that might be useful. "Why don't I give Stuart a call? He's had to deal with Vinny hanging around his tree lot for days on end. Maybe he's heard Vinny say something that would be a clue about what sort of hiding place Vinny would choose."

The idea was worth a shot, so I pulled out my phone and dialed up Stuart as Theo continued to drive in a somewhat aimless direction.

"Izzy!" Stuart shouted into the phone in greeting. He sounded horrified, and his voice was so loud that my ears were instantly ringing. I winced and pulled the phone away from my ear, putting him on speakerphone instead.

"Yes, it's Izzy. Why are you shouting? And how did you know it was me? I didn't know you had my number in your contacts list."

"I added it in from your customer contact form after you bought the tree, just in case I ever needed to call a good sleuth. But, Izzy! I need your help! I'm under attack!"

I glanced over at Theo, who was looking back at me with a worried expression on his face. He slowed his driving, and leaned over to talk to Stuart.

"Stuart, it's Theo Russo. I'm with Izzy at the moment. What's going on? Where are you, and who's attacking you?"

"I'm at my tree lot! It's Vinny! He's gone completely crazy. He's here with an axe, trying to chop all my trees to pieces!"

Theo swerved, making an immediate u-turn to head in the direction of Stuart's tree lot. "Hang on Stuart, we're coming. Stay out of his way, okay? I don't want you to get your head chopped off trying to save a tree. Have you called the police?"

"No," Stuart whimpered. "I've been too busy trying to chase Vinny down with my own axe. He can't just destroy my trees and expect to get away with it!"

My eyes widened. "Oh, this is not good! Someone is going to end up dead, and it might be Stuart!"

Theo glanced into the backseat for a moment. "Scott, call the police and tell them to head to the tree lot." Then he turned to yell back into my phone, which I was gripping so tightly between us that my knuckles were turning white. "Stuart, just stay out of Vinny's way! He's a dangerous murderer, and I don't want you to be the next one he takes out. We're on our way to help you, and so are the police."

There were several moments of loud shuffling, and then Stuart spoke into the receiver again. "I can't talk anymore. I have to go stop him. Come help as soon as you can!"

With that, the line went dead. Theo and I looked at each other for one long, horrified beat, and then Theo turned his eyes back to the road and floored his accelerator.

A few moments later, Scott shouted out that the police were on their way, but by then Theo was almost at the tree lot. We would beat the cops, and I wasn't sure if that was a good thing. If Vinny was swinging an axe around, what kind of gruesome scene might we encounter? Stuart was just stubborn enough that he might put himself between that axe and a Christmas tree, and end up with his face split wide open.

But when we screeched into the parking lot, I was relieved to see Stuart running toward us with his face still very much intact. He was waving his hands over his head and shouting something incoherent. I hopped out of the car and ran toward him, eager to make sure he was alright. I felt a wave of guilt wash over me as I saw his distraught expression. I couldn't believe that I'd ever thought that he was the murderer. Mitch had been right. There was no way this sweet old man would ever have killed anyone in cold blood.

"He's gone!" Stuart shrieked, finally saying something I could understand. Behind me, Theo, Scott and Molly also ran up to see whether Stuart was okay. Sprinkles ran in excited circles around us, barking at the top of his lungs.

"Gone?" I repeated, my eyes wide. This was good news for Stuart, but bad news for us and the cops. Where had Vinny gone now?

I was about to ask Stuart if he knew, but I didn't even need to say the question aloud. Stuart was on a roll now, excitedly waving his hands around as he explained what had happened.

"I got so angry at that fool that I chased him down with a chainsaw!" he exclaimed.

Theo choked in surprise. "You did *what*?"

Stuart nodded vigorously. "You heard me. I got out my power chainsaw and went running after him. I've had enough of him hanging around here and bothering my customers, and now trying to chop my trees up because he thinks I hate the environment. I don't hate it! I love Mother Earth! He just won't stop to listen for two seconds and understand that my trees aren't actually bad for the environment."

"Did you get him with the chainsaw?" I asked, almost afraid to know the answer. I was picturing Vinny running off with a horrible wound, bleeding to death. But Stuart was shaking his head.

"No, he saw me coming and took off like the coward that he is. He hopped into his car and zoomed off, yelling that he'd be back to deal with me later."

"Did he say where he was going?" Molly asked.

Stuart nodded, bobbing his head up and down like it was being shaken by hurricane-force winds. "He was yelling something about getting Colleen. I'm afraid he's going to go take the axe to the decorations in her yard. Or worse, to her!"

"Why didn't you say so in the first place?" Scott yelped out in exasperation. He reached for his phone to call 911 again and let the cops know that they would need to switch directions to head for Colleen's house.

"We've gotta go!" Theo said to Stuart, who looked completely dazed and confused at this point. I felt badly for him, as he'd obviously been through quite an ordeal in the last half hour, but we didn't have time to stop and make him feel better right now. We needed to get to Colleen's and stop Vinny before he harmed her.

I'd barely shut the door to the passenger side of Theo's car before he was speeding off again. As I struggled to buckle myself in, I felt a sense of dread rising within me once more. I was relieved that Stuart hadn't been harmed by Vinny's axe, but I was worried that Colleen wasn't going to be so lucky.

As Theo sped onto Colleen's street, I could see that Vinny's car was parked right in the middle of her yard. It looked like he'd driven straight into a lighted gingerbread house, and his front windshield was now decorated with a sugar plum fairy.

"He's gone completely insane!" Molly exclaimed.

"Yeah, he's wrecked his car on that gingerbread house," Scott agreed. "Why does he even have a car, anyway? Isn't that bad for the environment. It doesn't look like it's the most fuel-efficient vehicle."

I peered at Vinny's car, which indeed looked like an old clunker that probably spewed more than its fair share of carbon into the atmosphere every time he turned it on. "I'm sure he has some explanation for why his car isn't that bad," I said. "But I don't care about that right now. We need to see if Colleen is in there!"

As Theo came to another screeching halt, this time in Colleen's driveway, I saw that Vinny was standing on her front porch and swinging his axe at her front door over and over. For a moment, we all sat in stunned silence. Then, Theo leapt into action.

"Scott, come with me," he ordered. "Izzy and Molly, you ladies stay in the car. I don't want you tangled up in this. That man is dangerous."

But Molly was already jumping out of the backseat. "Not on your life, Theo. I'm not standing by watching you and Scott get chopped to pieces. Besides, I have a secret weapon up my sleeve."

As she ran off, with Sprinkles running after her and once again barking at the top of his lungs, I saw her pull a vial of pepper spray out of her purse.

"Molly carries pepper spray?" Theo asked. "In Sunshine Springs? Who's going to attack her here?"

But no one answered him. Scott had already leapt out of the car to run after his fiancée, screaming at her to stay away from Vinny. As for me, I'd seen Molly's vial of pepper spray before. She'd proudly shown it to me when she'd first purchased it, and had informed me that it was the maximum size and strength legally allowed by the state of California. I wasn't worried about her safety. She was going to take Vinny down with that stuff, no doubt.

I was, however, worried about Sprinkles. He had no idea what Auntie Molly was about to do, and I didn't want him to get caught in the crossfire of the spray while trying to valiantly protect her. I jumped out of the car and ran after him, yelling at him to follow me but knowing that he probably wasn't going to listen. He could be impossibly hardheaded, especially when he thought that one of the humans he loved needed protection.

"Molly! Wait! Let me get Sprinkles!" I shouted. Thankfully, she heard me and turned to nod in my direction.

"Hurry!" she called out. "Vinny's almost through the door."

Vinny wasn't paying any attention to us. He was completely focused on getting through Colleen's front door, which was now quite splintered. He probably only needed two or three more good hits and he'd be inside her house. I wasn't sure why he didn't just smash the glass on the floor-to-ceiling windows on either side of the door. That seemed like a much easier way to get in. But he obviously wasn't thinking clearly, and I was glad of that. His decision to go for the door had bought us all just enough time to stop him before he got to Colleen.

At least, I hoped it had.

I dove for Sprinkles, grabbing him by his red and green Christmas collar and dragging him off the porch. The bells on the collar jingled merrily, a jolly noise that seemed quite out of place in the current moment. He whined in protest, and I gave him a sharp look.

"I swear, Sprinkles. You're too stubborn for your own good. If I wasn't such a softie I would have let you stay up there by Molly. Trust me, that would have taught you to never again ignore me when I call you."

Sprinkles, still not understanding the gravity of the situation, only whined again. I looked up to see Molly raising the vial of pepper spray and pointing it in Vinny's direction. Then, to my horror, I realized that Scott was still standing much too close.

"Scott! Back up!" I yelled. "That stuff is strong! You're way too close!"

Scott ignored me and kept moving closer, determined to protect Molly. Thankfully, Theo had realized what was going on by now, and was running up to the porch at that very moment. He tackled Scott, sending both of them tumbling down the stairs and off the porch at the exact moment that Molly let loose a long stream of pepper spray in Vinny's direction.

For a few moments, it felt like time stood still. I watched Molly shield her own eyes, then run off the porch as soon as she'd sprayed Vinny. Vinny, who had still been singularly focused on chopping down the door, dropped his axe and let out an inhuman-sounding howl. He put his hands up to his face and rolled around on the ground, screaming that he was blinded.

"Does that stuff really blind people?" Theo asked. He and Scott had rolled to a stop not far from where Sprinkles and I were sitting, and they were both staring up at Vinny with concern.

"Only temporarily," Molly said as she walked up to us, looking quite pleased with herself. The blindness will last about fifteen minutes, plenty of time for the cops to get here and arrest him."

Sprinkles whined again, this time in an apologetic sort of way. He looked up at me sheepishly, as if acknowledging that it had indeed been a good idea to stay out of the way. I ruffled his ears and kissed the top of his muzzle, forgiving him instantly. I couldn't be mad at him when I knew he had only been trying to protect Molly. I was just glad he was okay.

And I was glad that Vinny had been caught. I saw Colleen's horrified face peeking through the glass of her front windows, and I gave her a small wave to reassure her that everything was okay now.

As if on cue, I heard the wail of police sirens. The police would be here in just a few minutes. Vinny would be arrested, and the "Christmas Curse" would be lifted. Another murderer would be off the streets. I saw Molly reaching for her cell phone, and I laughed. I knew she was getting ready to take another selfie with Vinny being arrested in the background. She had quite a collection of selfies with murderers being arrested behind her, and this would perhaps be the sweetest one yet. Sunshine Springs could truly enjoy the holiday season now.

Or so I thought.

As Vinny writhed around on the porch, wailing in pain, he managed to get out a few coherent sentences that made my blood run cold.

"I'm not the murderer!" he yelled. "Why can't anyone get that through their head? I didn't kill Simon. Colleen did it, and I can prove it!"

Theo, Molly, Scott and I all looked at each other in confused shock as the police cars sped down Colleen's street.

CHAPTER SEVENTEEN

As soon as the squad cars were parked, the Sunshine Springs deputies launched themselves out of their vehicles like their behinds were on fire. What followed was mass confusion. Everyone seemed to be talking at once as the officers asked what happened and we tried to explain it. One of the officers went to check on Vinny, and called in to have a paramedic check on him, just in case. No one bothered to cuff him just yet. He was still writhing around in pain, and clearly wasn't going to be escaping anywhere anytime soon.

He continued to shout about Colleen being guilty, but no one paid that much attention to him. After the initial shock of hearing him say that, I realized that he was just trying to cast the blame off of himself in any way he could. He couldn't really expect anyone to believe that he wasn't the criminal here after the way he'd been acting all night.

Molly and I explained to the officers that we had reason to believe that Vinny had faked a tattoo to frame Lynette for the vandalism to Simon's yard. We also told them about how he'd been going crazy down at Stuart's just a half hour earlier, trying to take down the tree lot with his axe until Stuart chased him off with a chainsaw. And then, of course, the evidence of his outlandish attempt to break into Colleen's house was right in front of us. I glanced at the door and shivered. It hung in about a thousand splintered pieces, and if we hadn't arrived when we had, who knows what Vinny would have done to Colleen.

Thinking of Colleen made me wonder where she was. She had disappeared after her brief peek out the window, and I supposed I couldn't blame her. She was probably terrified after nearly having a psycho murderer break into her house.

Vinny, for his part, was still ranting about Colleen being guilty. The paramedics had arrived by now, and he was sitting up on the porch. He had stopped writhing around, and was allowing the medical staff to wipe his face down with something to alleviate the pepper spray burns. Even from a distance, I could see that his face had swelled quite a bit, but it looked like he was at least able to see once again. One of the officers had gone to stand by him now, just in case he got any ideas about trying to make a run for it.

Molly, Theo, Scott and I had finished telling the officers everything we knew, and so they decided to go knock on what was left of the door and see if Colleen was ready to make a statement. They also wanted to check that she was alright. To say that she'd had a bit of a fright was quite an understatement.

I sighed, feeling strangely dissatisfied. The murderer had been found, and would likely be officially arrested in a few moments once the paramedics were done with him. But I didn't feel the same exuberance I'd felt when other murder cases had been solved. Was it because Vinny hadn't officially confessed? Usually, by the time the police came to arrest the criminal I'd been chasing down, that criminal had broken down and admitted to everything they'd done. But despite the strong evidence against Vinny, and despite the fact that he'd attacked Lynette, Mitch, Stuart and Colleen tonight, he was still claiming that he wasn't the one responsible for Simon's death. He couldn't expect anyone to actually believe him, could he?

Apparently, he did. He was yelling at the officer that they'd have to believe him when he showed them the evidence he'd found.

"He's delusional, right?" Theo asked, glancing in my direction. "There's no evidence against Colleen, is there?"

I frowned. "Not that I know of. Mitch was pretty open with me about what evidence he'd discovered on this case, and he never mentioned anything about Colleen. I mean, she has been acting a bit weird. She had that big party just after Simon died, which seems like a strange thing for a grieving widow to do. But I wrote that off as her grieving in her own way."

Scott started to speak, but he was interrupted by a sudden exclamation from Molly.

"Look! Is that Colleen?"

We all turned to look in the direction that Molly was pointing, and I saw that the woman she was pointing at did indeed look like Colleen. It was hard to say for sure, because the figure was running through the shadows and was wearing a dark hoodie, but the height and build looked about right to be Colleen.

Alarm bells went off in my head. Was there actually something to what Vinny was saying? Why would Colleen be running if she had nothing to hide?

At that moment, the running figure turned to look, obviously startled by Molly's loud exclamation. I gasped when the flashing lights from the police cars illuminated her face, and I saw that it was indeed Colleen. Theo, Scott, and Molly saw it too.

"Um...why is she running away?" Molly asked, her voice taking on a skeptical tone.

None of us answered out loud, but we didn't have to. Suspicion hung heavy in the air. If Colleen was innocent, why was she running away from her own home? If she was the victim here, why was she trying to escape?

She stared back at us for a few moments, frozen in fright, and then she turned and kept running. The police officers hadn't noticed her. They were too busy dealing with Vinny and the mess he'd made of the front yard and house. But I realized in that moment that Vinny was right. I didn't know what proof he had, and I definitely didn't think he was an innocent party here. He'd destroyed Colleen's entire front yard, and her door—not to mention what he'd done to Lynette's house, Stuart's tree lot, and Mitch's leg. Yet he was not the one who had murdered Simon.

I should have seen it clearer before now. I had automatically given Colleen the benefit of the doubt, since she was a grieving widow. But everything at her Christmas party had been too weird. People didn't just throw merry, giant parties days after their spouse had died.

Another thought flashed across my mind in that instant. She had arrived at the scene of Simon's murder very soon after his body was discovered. She'd claimed that it was because news of his death was already spreading, but I'd always found it a bit remarkable just how quickly the news had spread, and how fast she'd made it over from the party she'd been supposedly attending back to the location of Simon's murder. It had almost been as if she'd had some sort of foreknowledge that he was dead—which made sense if she was the one who'd killed him.

And now, she was running. She must have realized how close she was getting to having her whole scheme revealed, and she was trying to escape before someone blamed her for the murder.

I felt a rush of anger rising within me until I was sure there must be smoke coming out of my ears. She was the one who had caused all of the tourists to fear Sunshine Springs. Her heartless murder of her husband had been the spark that set off the newspaper firestorm about the supposed Christmas curse. I didn't know all of the details about how or why she would kill her own spouse, but I knew with certainty in that moment that she had done it.

And I wasn't going to let her get away with it.

"Stop her!" I shouted, taking off at a full-on sprint in the direction she was running. "Stop Colleen! She's the murderer!"

I could see the officers scattered across the yard looking up at me in confusion. They barely got out of my way before I barreled past them. Behind me, I heard Vinny yelling that finally someone around here was talking some sense. His comments annoyed me—I definitely didn't need praise from a scoundrel like him, and I had my own beef with him over the way he'd treated Mitch and Stuart. But that could be saved for another moment. Right now, all that mattered was catching Colleen.

I wasn't in the best shape of my life, and it certainly didn't help things that I'd been eating so much holiday pie lately. But I pushed myself as hard as I could, propelling forward on pure adrenaline. Luckily, Colleen didn't seem to be an expert runner, either. She shrieked as she ran, occasionally looking over her shoulder to see whether I was gaining on her. I was, and her glances backward only slowed her further. After only a few minutes of pursuit, I caught up with her and tackled her.

"Get your filthy, pie-flour hands off of me!" she shouted, trying to wriggle away. I kept a firm hold on her, however, and she wasn't able to get up off the ground. Less than a minute after I'd tackled her, Theo, Scott, Molly, and several police officers caught up with me. Sprinkles showed up as well, running in wild circles around me and growling viciously at Colleen.

"Get your mangy mutt away from me!" Colleen yelled, but no one was listening to her.

The officers who had shown up looked from me to Colleen, apparently unsure of what to do.

"Izzy?" one of them finally asked. "What's going on here?"

"I'm holding down your murderer, waiting for one of you to get out some cuffs and arrest her," I said. "I'd appreciate it if you'd hurry up. This is like trying to hold a cat down in a tub of water."

"You're sure she's the murderer?" the officer asked.

I groaned in exasperation, and I saw Theo give the officer a firm push in my direction.

"Izzy knows her stuff," he said gruffly. "If she says there's a reason to arrest Colleen, then you'd do well to arrest her."

Colleen started screaming obscenities, and saying that I didn't know anything. But Theo's encouragement was enough for the officer, and he put cuffs on Colleen. I stood up, panting from exertion, to see that Molly was just finishing taking a selfie on her phone.

"Don't tell me I was in that picture!" I said.

Molly laughed merrily. "You are! Look, I got several action shots. There's nothing like a selfie with your best friend in the background, wrestling down a murderer so the police can make an arrest."

She held her phone up to show me, but I scowled at her and swatted it away. "Ugh, I don't want to see. I must look like a complete mess right now. I've got grass and dirt and leaves all over me, and my hair is a ball of tangles."

"You look lovely," Theo insisted.

I scowled at him, too, then turned on my heel and started following the officer who had handcuffed Colleen. He was dragging her, kicking and screaming, back in the direction of her house.

When we all arrived back in Colleen's yard, the officer in charge angrily asked what was going on. I could tell he was stressed out to the max. Usually, Mitch was in charge of cases this serious. If Mitch couldn't be there for some reason, then Officer Smith, the second-most senior officer in the police force, would take over. But Officer Smith was on vacation, and Sheriff Mitch was in the hospital, so this poor officer was stuck dealing with the chaotic climax of the most complicated murder case Sunshine Springs had seen yet. I couldn't help feeling a bit sympathetic toward him.

"Colleen Farrington murdered her husband, Simon Farrington," I explained. Before I could continue my explanation, Colleen started shrieking that she had done no such thing, while Vinny cheered, once again exclaiming with pleasure that someone was finally smart enough to listen to him.

"Enough!" the head officer bellowed at the top of his lungs. "Everyone be quiet and let Izzy speak, or I swear I'll throw all of you in jail right now!"

The officer's threat seemed credible enough that everyone calmed down. I took a deep breath and started speaking, wondering how much I was going to be able to say before Colleen started screaming again. She was staring daggers at me, and I had no doubts that she would have liked nothing more in that moment than to literally tear my head off. Her anger only confirmed for me that she was the murderer. Innocent people didn't rage in the way she was currently raging.

"I don't know what proof Vinny has," I said. "But I do know that Colleen is guilty."

As quickly as I could, I explained that Colleen had arrived at the scene of Simon's murder a little too quickly, and that her party just after his death showed that she was not the grieving widow she was trying to portray herself as.

"That doesn't mean anything!" Colleen spat out, unable to hold her silence any longer. "Simon would have wanted me to have that party. He loved Christmas, and he wouldn't have wanted my spirits to be dampened by cancelling that party!"

A loud snort of laughter startled me from behind. I turned to see, to my great shock, that Lynette was standing there.

"What are *you* doing here?" Colleen roared out.

Lynette crossed her arms. "I came to warn you that Vinny was rampaging around again. He came to my house earlier and destroyed a bunch of my decorations. After I recovered from the shock of that, I realized that he might be heading here next. And as much as I don't like you and didn't like Simon, I do have some kind bones in my body. I thought it would be pretty awful for you to have to deal with another round of vandalism in the middle of everything else that's already going on. But maybe I shouldn't be so nice to you. What Izzy's saying makes perfect sense."

"You see!" Vinny shouted, struggling in vain to free himself from the officers who were holding him down. "It's true. Even Lynette sees it!"

Lynette turned to glare at Vinny. "I don't think anyone asked you to speak. I see you've been arrested, which is good. You've caused enough trouble yourself tonight."

I saw Vinny's eyes darken, and I could tell that he was about to yell at Lynette. I didn't want this situation to devolve into a shouting match between Lynette, Vinny, and Colleen, so I quickly jumped in to interrupt.

"Lynette, were you aware of any tension between Simon and Colleen?"

Lynette snorted again. "Of course. Anyone who knew them was. Colleen and Simon hated each other. They only stayed together because it would have been so expensive to divorce. They had an agreement where each one let the other do what they wanted. A 'live and let live' sort of thing. Colleen allowed Simon to have his decorations, and he allowed her to attend and throw her wild parties. As long as they stayed out of each other's way, everything was fine."

"She's full of it!" Colleen shouted. "She doesn't know what she's talking about. Simon and I had a loving relationship that was cut too short by a senseless act of violence!"

The officer holding Colleen gave her a stern look to silence her. "Keep quiet, or you're going straight to jail."

Reluctantly, Colleen clamped her mouth shut as Lynette continued.

"Colleen hated Simon's decorations, but, like I said, she tolerated them because he tolerated her parties. I never put two and two together before, but after hearing you speak, Izzy, it all makes perfect sense. Simon was in a rush this year, trying to get his decorations up before anyone. But he couldn't get ahead because Vinny here was following him around, pestering him and destroying his work. Simon got desperate and asked Colleen to help him. I know that because she complained nonstop about it to anyone who would listen. Word around town was that she was unbearable at parties because all she did was complain about Simon."

"That's not true! You're just jealous because you don't get invited to parties like I do!"

Another stern look from the police officer silenced Colleen, although I noticed she was looking paler by the moment. Lynette's explanations were making her nervous.

"Oh, I'm not jealous of you, especially not since you're about to be headed to jail for life." Lynette tried to toss her short hair over her shoulder haughtily. "I see exactly what happened. You found out Simon was cheating on the contest, and decided it was the perfect way to scare him into showing up on Main Street so you could murder him."

"It's true!" Vinny piped in. "That's what I've been trying to tell you all. I found the magazines in her trash can that have all the letters and words cut out from them. She's such an idiot that she just threw them away!"

I looked over at Vinny in surprise. It did sound like he might have found some actual evidence, albeit in an unconventional way. "What in the world were you doing sifting through Colleen's trash can?" I asked.

He rolled his eyes. "Looking for recyclable material, of course. Colleen never bothered to separate her recyclables from her trash. She prefers to kill Mother Earth, like so many of you."

"You can't prove that anything is from me!" Colleen shouted. "If there are magazines there, then you planted them."

Vinny looked at her smugly. "Unfortunately for you, I'm smart, and only touched the very first magazine I saw. When I realized what I was looking at, I left the rest undisturbed. None of them will have my fingerprints on them, but I bet they'll have *your* fingerprints on them."

This was too much for Colleen, she started screaming and trying to lunge for Vinny. The officers tried to calm her down but she refused to listen to reason. We all stared at the circus unfolding in front of us, unsure of what to say or do. Finally Molly leaned over to me and whispered, "Can you even pull fingerprints from a magazine page?"

I shrugged. "Not sure. But it looks like the idea of doing so has Colleen quite worried."

At that moment, Colleen finally broke down. The pressure of the evidence mounting against her was too much to take, and she burst into sobs.

"Okay, okay, so I made the letter. I had found out that Simon was cheating on the decorating contest, and I thought that wasn't right. But he wouldn't listen to me when I told him to stop, so I made the letter to put the fear of God in him. I just wanted to scare him a bit. I was planning to hide a short distance away on Main Street and watch him sweat a bit while he waited for the mystery blackmailer. I never imagined he'd be killed that night, or I wouldn't have done it! I know he and Vinny were fighting that night! Vinny must have taken advantage of the fact that he was out there alone and strangled him!"

Vinny laughed in a maniacal tone. "I didn't kill him. Yeah, I fought with him that night. But I'm out to save the environment, not murder people and land myself in jail. Unlike some people, I do know where to draw the line."

I was tempted to tell him that he did not, in fact, know where to draw the line. He had gone quite far across the line when he vandalized property, caused Mitch to get into a wreck, and took an axe to Stuart's tree lot. But that was a discussion for another time. For now, I was interested in untangling the details of Simon's murder.

The police officer in charge looked helplessly back and forth between Vinny and Colleen. "I'd say there's evidence against both of you. I'm going to have to take you both in and do further interrogation to determine who the actual murderer was."

I glanced over at Lynette, who was shaking her head in disgust. "They're both awful human beings," she declared. "For all I know they worked together to kill him."

Vinny seemed genuinely offended by this suggestion. "I did no such thing! I would never work together with Colleen on anything! She's the awful one here!"

I frowned as I mulled over all the details I'd just learned about the case. The officers were struggling to cuff Colleen, and in a few moments both Colleen and Vinny would be loaded into the back of squad cars to take them to the station. Progress had been made on the case, yes. But I was still disappointed that I hadn't been able to figure out a definitive answer to who had murdered Simon.

But then, like a lightning bolt, the truth hit me.

"Of course!" I said with a laugh. "Why didn't I see it before?"

Everyone paused and turned to look at me.

"See what?" one of the officers prompted.

"Colleen is the murderer, and I'll tell you why. She just did herself in by contradicting her own testimony."

"What are you talking about?" Scott asked. Beside him, Molly and Theo also looked confused.

"She said she just wanted to scare Simon, so she made a blackmail letter to send him to Main Street and make him sweat."

"Yeah..." Theo said, sounding confused about where I was going with this.

"But if she had actually been there, hiding out to watch him 'sweat,' she would have seen the moment he was murdered."

Understanding dawned on everyone's faces, except Colleen's. Her face was covered in panic.

"I left early to go to a party!" she claimed. "I watched him sweat for a moment, and then I left to go enjoy time with my friends. I already told Mitch that that's where I was that night."

I shook my head. "No, you told Mitch you were running late to the party because you'd helped Simon fix some of his decorations. But that doesn't make sense. Simon was downtown long before your party started. You would have had plenty of time to get ready and get to the party on time. You know what I think the truth is? I think you originally planned to just make Simon sweat. But then, after he insisted you help him fix his decorations, you finally lost it. You two had hated each other for some time, I'd warrant. When you saw him on Main Street, and saw Vinny

123

fighting with him, you decided it was the perfect time to take him out."

"I have no idea what you're implying," Colleen said in a huff.

"Then let me explain," I said, feeling smug. "You waited until Theo had broken up the fight between Vinny and Simon, and then, when the coast was clear, you approached Simon. He was already rattled, and he must have been even more rattled when he saw you. He was probably afraid that you were going to catch him in the middle of meeting with his blackmailer. You took advantage of his confusion and strangled him. As much as you two fought, he must have still been quite shocked to realize his own wife was suffocating him. By the time he realized what was going on, it was too late. He was already too weak to fight back, and you killed him."

"This is absurd!" Colleen exclaimed. "Is anyone else hearing how ridiculous this all sounds?"

No one else seemed to think what I was saying was absurd. They all leaned in with great interest to hear what I had to say next.

"You sped away to get to the Christmas party as fast as you could. It was the almost perfect alibi. If you got there quickly enough, it would seem as though you had been already almost at the party at the time of Simon's death. Surely, you had just been driving along innocently while someone else strangled him, right? But no, you were driving like a maniac to place yourself far away from the crime scene as quickly as possible. You knew you could easily blame Vinny, because he'd been seen by more than one witness fighting with Simon. And you had the added insurance of having security footage of Lynette vandalizing your yard, so you could always fall back on blaming her."

"I did not vandalize this yard!" Lynette cried out indignantly.

I looked over at her and nodded. "I know. Vinny did. He had a fake tattoo and was impersonating you."

"What?" Vinny cried out. "That's ridiculous!"

I held up my hand for him to be silent. "Save it for the judge. You're in a whole lot of trouble for all of your own bad behavior. But you're actually quite lucky, because all of that bad behavior almost landed you on trial for murder. Your hatred for Simon almost let Colleen kill him without being caught. But she was a bit too sloppy, and now she's going to have to answer for what she's done."

That was the moment that Colleen seemed to realize that she'd been found out. She started screaming hysterically, yelling that she'd had no choice but to kill Simon because he'd been so awful to live with. I merely nodded in satisfaction as they dragged her away.

"They all break down in the end," I mused. "A heavy conscience is too great a weight to bear."

"Quick!" Molly exclaimed, and dragged me, Scott and Theo into a group hug. "Let's take a group selfie."

Her arm wasn't long enough to get all of us in the picture and still have Colleen in the background, so Scott took the phone and managed to get a decent enough shot. I could only laugh as she scrolled through to look at the photos.

"Looks like you have quite a few interesting selfies documenting tonight."

Molly flashed a brilliant smile in my direction. "This is going to be my best update to my selfies album yet."

Forensics had arrived by then, and was shooing us off the lawn so they could document the mess and hopefully find the supposed magazines in Colleen's trash can. That was fine by me. I didn't want to hang around this place any longer, and I didn't think anyone else did, either. Sprinkles wagged his tail like crazy as we started walking back toward Theo's car.

My phone buzzed, and I looked down to see that I had a text from Alice. I smiled in relief as I read it. "Mitch is in stable condition," I announced. "He has a broken leg, but other than that he only suffered some minor scrapes."

"Thank God," Theo said. "Should we run by the hospital to visit him?"

"Definitely," Molly said. "Maybe we should stop by Izzy's café to grab some pie for him first. That will cheer him up."

"Sounds like a plan to me," I agreed. "But I hope you don't all think it's rude of me to be on the phone while we're riding over. I have a few important phone calls to make."

They all looked at me with curiosity. "Phone calls?" Scott asked. "Who could you possibly need to call so urgently at the moment?"

I smiled, savoring the happy relief I felt as I explained. "I have a few news reporters I need to call. I think they might be very interested in getting the inside scoop on the resolution of Simon's murder case. Of course, I'm sure that in exchange for that inside scoop, they'll be more than happy to report that the Christmas Curse in Sunshine Springs has been lifted."

Theo laughed, and pulled me into a big bear hug. "You did it, Izzy. You saved Christmas!"

I couldn't help feeling warm and safe in his embrace. And he was right: Christmas was saved, although I couldn't take full credit for it. I'd had plenty of help along the way. But I didn't care who got the recognition for solving Simon's murder case. I only cared that this was indeed going to be the best holiday season ever.

CHAPTER EIGHTEEN

*** *About Three Weeks Later* * * *

I stepped back to survey the long table that I'd set up in the middle of the Drunken Pie Café, and I nodded with satisfaction. I had done a fantastic job of transforming the café into a Christmas wonderland, if I did say so myself. Of course, I'd already done a great deal of decorating before tonight. Lighted garlands, bright red bows, and shimmering snowflakes adorned the ceiling, and around the room an occasional gingerbread man, reindeer, or giant candy cane figurine could be seen. The large Christmas tree that I'd bought from Stuart stood magnificently in the corner, although I couldn't help feeling a bit sheepish every time I looked at it. It made me think of my ridiculous attempt to get it inside by myself.

But the trouble that tree had caused had been worth it, because all of the tourists had loved it. They had come in droves to ooh and ahh over its adorned branches—and I do mean droves. After the newspapers reported that Simon's murder had been a lovers' quarrel and not a Christmas Curse, the tourists had been more eager than ever to make it by Sunshine Springs. They had happily indulged in holiday treats and wine, and bought souvenirs until all of the Sunshine Springs business owners thought we might literally pass out from happy exhaustion. We were all going to head into the New Year with our bills paid and savings replenished.

But now, it was five p.m. on Christmas Eve, and all the tourists had gone home. Sunshine Springs was quiet, and although there wasn't snow in our mild Northern California climate, Main Street looked quite festive to make up for it.

The table I'd just set looked festive as well. I'd set ten place settings, which was a few more than I needed. But whenever I had friends for dinner at the café, I inevitably ended up with a few more guests than I'd invited. It was a happy problem to have, and I had learned to just make sure that I planned for a few extra seats.

A sharp rap on the door drew my attention, and I looked up to see Grams standing outside, balancing a giant stack of gift boxes in her arms. Sprinkles raised his head from the spot where he'd been snoozing behind the giant Christmas tree, and barked with excitement when he realized it was her. He ran to the door and didn't stop barking until I had opened it for her.

"Grams! What's all this?"

"Oh, nothing much. Just a few presents for everyone who's coming tonight."

"This is more than a few!"

Grams set the presents down under the tree and looked up with a grin. "I might have gotten a teensy bit carried away."

I shook my head and laughed. What else could I do?

Grams busied herself arranging the presents, her neon pink hair shimmering under the twinkling lights. About a week ago, she'd given up on the red and green hair, saying that it wasn't bright enough for her, even if it was festive. She'd declared herself a sugar plum fairy from the Nutcracker's land of sweets instead, and she did sort of look like a fairy. A very bright, neon-colored fairy, but a fairy nonetheless. Her bright purple dress glittered brilliantly, and her layers of multicolored, beaded necklaces completed the look. She just needed some wings and she'd be a true fairy.

Another rap at the door sounded, and I turned to see quite a group standing outside. Scott and Molly were there, standing arm and arm beside Alice, who had her hand protectively on Mitch's back. Mitch was on crutches, and still had a few weeks before the cast on his leg came off. But overall, he was healing up nicely. He certainly wasn't complaining about the fact that Alice had been doting over him while he recovered. I went to let them in, giving everyone warm hugs of greeting.

"Grams is already here," I said. "Go inside and make yourselves comfortable."

Before I could turn around to follow them, I saw Theo walking down the sidewalk, chatting amiably with Sophia, Sunshine Springs' favorite hairdresser.

"Hi, Theo," I said in a teasing voice. Did you just come from an appointment to get your nails done?"

Sophia laughed, but Theo rolled his eyes at me.

"If you must know, I ran into Sophia while I was at the grocery store, picking this up for you." He held out a beautiful potted poinsettia plant.

I gasped. "It's gorgeous. I've never seen one this nice from the grocery store! Poinsettias are my favorite!"

"I know. Your Grams told me. And I looked over every last plant in that store to make sure I got you the best one. Merry Christmas, Izzy."

I grinned up at him. "Thank you. Merry Christmas."

Then I looked over at Sophia. "Let me guess, Theo invited you to tag along to our little dinner here?"

Sophia nodded, suddenly looking flustered. "I hope that's okay! I don't want to intrude, but my flight home to my parents was delayed. I'm stuck here alone for Christmas, and Theo promised you wouldn't mind."

"I don't mind at all," I said, reaching to give her a hug while being careful not to smash the poinsettia. "Come on in. The more the merrier."

"Did I hear someone say the more the merrier?" a familiar voice asked. I turned to see Moe, from Moe's souvenir shop next door, walking up with his fingers intertwined with Tiffany's. I raised an eyebrow at Tiffany. She'd been working hard for me at the café over the last several weeks, but she'd never mentioned she had started dating anyone, let alone Moe from the shop next door. She must have realized my surprise, and she gave me a sheepish shrug.

"I didn't want to say anything until I knew that we were actually serious about dating. But we've decided to be an official couple. Is it alright if he joins for the dinner?"

I smiled and gave her a big hug. "Of course! I mean it when I say the more the merrier. All of you get inside so we can start eating. I'm starving!"

I went back inside, my heart feeling full and happy. I started pouring wine into the glasses at the table, which was a surefire way to get everyone to sit down. A few minutes later, everyone was sitting in front of a festive place setting, drinking merrily as I passed around dishes of food. I hadn't wanted to work on Christmas Eve day, so I'd closed the café and spent the day cooking and baking. It had been worth it. My mouth watered at all the delicious smells filling the room, and from the way everyone was eagerly piling food onto their plates, their mouths were watering, too.

"Don't stuff yourselves too much," I warned. "There'll be pie for dessert, of course."

Everyone ignored me and continued piling their plates high, but that was fine by me. We'd all overeat tonight, I was sure. But what was a holiday if you didn't overeat?

Not long after we settled into eating, the conversation turned to Mitch's leg.

"How are you recovering, dear?" Grams asked.

Mitch cracked his knuckles and took a swig of wine before answering. "As well as can be expected. I'm back at the office this week, and that's a good thing. Things are a bit backed up."

"Has Colleen been officially charged?" Moe asked.

Mitch nodded. "Yeah. She gave a full confession, and now it'll be up to the judge to decide her sentence. But at least Simon's case is officially closed."

"What about Vinny?" I asked. "Did he confess to all of his crimes?"

Mitch laughed. "He's a lot more stubborn. But when we turned up evidence of his fake tattoo supplies, he finally caved. He was the vandal, and he'll have to answer for those crimes, as well as for a hit-and-run involving a police officer. He's in a heap of hot water, and is going to do his own share of time behind bars."

"I bet Stuart is glad about that," Sophia piped in to say. "When I went to buy a Christmas tree for the salon a few weeks ago, he was so stressed out about Vinny harassing him."

"Yeah, I think quite a few people were stressed out by Vinny," Tiffany said. "I'm glad he's not going to be running around town bothering people anymore. It's nice to care about the earth, but you can't use that as an excuse to act horribly toward people. And it's especially no excuse for causing a car accident!"

"I agree," Mitch said. "But like I said, I'm recovering nicely. It'll be a while before I'm able to get back in a squad car and patrol again, but at least I'm back at the office. I'm really lucky. Things could have been a lot worse."

Alice sighed. "They certainly could have! I'm just glad you're alright, pookie-bear."

Mitch's face turned red as Alice leaned over to give him a kiss. Most of us at the table tried to politely ignore Alice's over-the-top affection, but not Theo. He guffawed so hard he nearly fell out of his chair.

"Pookie-bear? Aw, Mitch, I did always think you were soft and cuddly."

"Shut up," Mitch growled. "You're just jealous because you don't have someone to call you pookie-bear."

Theo kept laughing, but I felt my own face heating up. Everyone at the table knew that if Theo had to choose someone to call him pookie-bear, it would be me. Not that I would ever use such a ridiculous nickname. That was more Alice's style. But the fact remained that I was uncomfortable with having the focus on Theo's relationship status, because that meant that everyone was pondering why I didn't want to date him. Quickly, I tried to change the subject.

"I think it's sweet that you two have found so much happiness with each other," I said loudly. "Is it possible there might be more wedding bells in the future than just Scott and Molly's?"

Mitch couldn't help but grin. "It's possible. But I'm not giving away all my secrets." He winked at Alice, and she blushed. I had a feeling there would be another couple engaged in Sunshine Springs before the New Year.

"Speaking of weddings," Scott said loudly. "Molly and I have finally set a date."

The whole table quieted and turned toward them with interest. Molly grinned. "March twenty-first, the first day of spring! Mark your calendars. I know it's a bit soon, but we've decided we want to keep things simple and just have a great, relaxing party with our friends. It doesn't have to be a big production to be a fairytale day."

She winked at me, and I smiled back at her. It seemed that everything was coming together at the end of the year exactly as it needed to. For the next hour, we all ate, drank, and laughed until our hearts and bellies were full. Then we spent another few hours opening presents, drinking egg nog, and eating a second round of pie. Molly gave me a framed collage of all of our "murderers being arrested" selfies, and I teared up a bit looking back at the memories.

"We had quite a year, didn't we?" I asked.

"Yes, and it wasn't even a full year, since you only moved here last May," Molly said. "Imagine how much fun we'll have next year, when we have a full twelve months to chase after criminals!"

Mitch groaned. "Can't you two at least stay out of trouble until my leg is healed?"

I winked at him. "No promises."

Everyone laughed, even Mitch. It was hard to be in a bad mood when surrounded by such good friends and family.

It was nearly midnight when everyone started finally saying their goodbyes. Grams tried to stay to help me clean up, but I waved her away.

"I know you'll be up early tomorrow to get things ready for Christmas breakfast. Let me take care of this. You go home and rest."

Ordinarily, she would have fought me on this, but Theo shooed her away, promising to help me. Grams, who had been not-so-subtly lobbying for me to date Theo, jumped at the opportunity to leave me alone with him, and hurried herself out the door.

I rolled my eyes at her retreating form. Theo and I were both tired. Even though the atmosphere in here was quite romantic, with the soft twinkling lights and smell of fresh pine, I was pretty sure we both just wanted to finish cleaning up and get home.

At least, that's what I told myself. I'd be lying if I said that the holiday atmosphere didn't make me feel a pang of loneliness. I'd pushed Theo away for so long, but why? He was an attractive, kind man, and we always had a lot of fun together. Was I only hurting myself by letting the hurts of the past keep me from the joys of the future?

I pushed those thoughts away. For once, Theo wasn't cracking jokes about wanting to date me, and I certainly wasn't going to bring it up. We worked in companionable silence, until the café was once again sparkling clean. I stood back and surveyed the space, smiling as I took in the beautiful decorations.

"What's this?" Theo asked, pointing to a stack of delivery boxes behind my counter. "It's not like you to let deliveries stack up."

"Oh, that. I ordered fully biodegradable takeout cups and containers to replace my less environmentally friendly ones. I just haven't had a chance to unpack them with all the holiday craziness this week."

Theo raised an eyebrow at me. "Did Vinny threaten to vandalize your café if you didn't switch?"

I laughed. "No, but he did make me think that I could be doing more to help the environment. It didn't cost much to switch, and it makes me feel good to know I'm helping in my own small way."

Theo walked around the counter to stand with me and survey the café. "Just don't take up Vinny's style of crusading."

I laughed. "I won't. Don't worry. I'll worry about my own actions and let everyone else worry about theirs."

"Good plan." Theo glanced at his watch, then glanced back at me, his eyes seeming to twinkle in the holiday lights. "Merry Christmas, Izzy. It's after midnight, so it's now officially the holiday."

I sighed happily. "Merry Christmas. It turned out to be a good one."

"Indeed. Thanks to you. You saved Christmas."

"With a lot of help."

"Don't sell yourself so short all the time. You've done a lot for Sunshine Springs in the short time you've been here. I hope you're planning to stay a long time."

I blushed, and couldn't help but notice how handsome he looked as he glanced over at me. "I'm not planning on ever leaving."

"Good. That's what I was hoping to hear."

And then, without warning, he leaned over and kissed me. I was so surprised that I didn't resist, and once I got over the shock of the moment, I was enjoying the kiss too much to pull away. I was instantly transported back to a balmy day under an orange tree by Theo's villa, where he'd come within seconds of kissing me. I'd been wondering since that day what it would feel like to have him kiss me, and now I knew. It felt fantastic.

And yet, I wasn't supposed to be doing this.

"Theo!" I said, pulling back suddenly. "What are you doing?"

He pointed above my head. "Just taking advantage of the mistletoe you finally hung in here."

I looked up, and, to my surprise, there was a big sprig of mistletoe above my head. "But I didn't put that there!"

Theo gave me a skeptical look. "It's your café, Izzy. Who else would have done it?"

And then, it hit me, and I started giggling. "Grams, of course. She knows this is my favorite spot in the café to stand. She put it there in hopes that I'd stand here and then you'd kiss me. She's been after me for the last few weeks to move on and open my heart again. She says Christmas is the perfect time to do that."

"And?" Theo asked softly. "Do you agree with her?"

I considered a moment, and then, with a nervous but excited heart, I nodded. "You know what? I do."

Theo kissed me again, and this time I didn't pull back first. When he finally stepped back to search my eyes, my heart felt like it was flying.

"Does this mean you're finally saying yes to dating me?"

I grinned. "Yes, on one condition."

"What's that?"

"You promise not to complain about my sleuthing, and you promise to share all the inside information on cases you get from Mitch."

Theo frowned. "That's two conditions."

I gave him an impish smile and shrugged. "That's my offer. Take it or leave it."

He threw back his head and laughed. "I'll take it. I would say that I hope there won't be any more reasons for you to sleuth in the future, but I know you. You'll always find adventures no matter what."

"Yes I will," I said as he pulled me into his arms. "But what would a small, wine-country town be without a few crazy adventures?"

"It wouldn't be home," he said. "That's for sure."

"No, it wouldn't," I agreed. "But thankfully, it is home, and there are lots of adventures to be had here. And now, we can have them together."

"I couldn't ask for a better Christmas gift," he replied.

Neither could I, my heart sang back. *Neither could I.*

ABOUT THE AUTHOR

Diana DuMont lives and writes in Northern California. When she's not reading or dreaming up her latest mystery plot, she can usually be found hiking in the nearby redwood forests. You can connect with her at www.dianadumont.com.

Made in the USA
Middletown, DE
29 November 2019